Jett

A SHADOW OPS TEAM NOVEL

Makenna Jameison

ISBN: 9798360887164

ALSO BY MAKENNA JAMEISON

ALPHA SEALS CORONADO

SEAL's Desire
SEAL's Embrace
SEAL's Honor
SEAL's Revenge
SEAL's Promise
SEAL's Redemption
SEAL's Command

Table of Contents

Chapter 1	1
Chapter 2	7
Chapter 3	25
Chapter 4	35
Chapter 5	41
Chapter 6	48
Chapter 7	65
Chapter 8	71
Chapter 9	77
Chapter 10	85
Chapter 11	96
Chapter 12	104
Chapter 13	111
Chapter 14	118
Chapter 15	127
Chapter 16	137
Chapter 17	147
Chapter 18	157
Chapter 19	163
Chapter 20	170
Epilogue	181
About the Author	185

Chapter 1

Jett Hutchinson sipped his whiskey, setting the glass down on the dark, polished bar. His gaze scanned the Friday evening crowd as conversations carried on around him in the dimly lit space. Damn Manhattan yuppies. With their suits and briefcases and designer shoes, they'd never fit in his world. They'd never want to. This crowd loved attention—money, power, success. He'd learned long ago to blend in anywhere. To slip through the shadows and move in on his target. No one paid him much attention tonight. He preferred it that way. He'd covertly infiltrated multiple locations around the world during his time in the Special Forces— of course that usually involved full combat gear and his finger on the trigger of his assault rifle, his teammates at his side. The U.S. Government at their backs.

This was a different type of subterfuge. More elegant. Practiced. But no less lethal in the end.

His target tonight didn't involve following his usual modus operandi. Nothing about this evening followed normal protocol. He might be waiting for a man, but he wasn't after blood. He needed cooperation. Loyalty. He needed someone he could trust.

Jett took another sip of the smooth whiskey, smirking as he watched some young Wall Street types bragging about their portfolios. Two young looking women were fawning over them, listening with bated breath. Real men never kissed and told. At forty-two, he wasn't exactly old, but he had more than a decade on those fresh-faced kids. He'd been out in the real world for twenty damn years—first in the military and then in his own line of work.

His former teammate Gray Pierce finally came in through the bar doors, his short beard reminding Jett of their days trekking through enemy territory. He'd kept in good shape since leaving the service. His broad shoulders filled out his shirt, and Jett noticed the way women looked at him as he crossed the room.

His lips quirked.

Gray probably wouldn't mind slipping into one of their beds tonight after Jett filled him in on his proposition. His carefully assembled team at Shadow Security could use another man, especially after that last ass wipe had bailed. Jett had doubts about him right from the start, and they'd proven right. He'd learned to always trust his gut, and going off course could've cost them everything. Gray was the man he needed.

"Shadow," Gray said with a smirk, his dark eyes showing his amusement.

Jett bristled slightly. He'd served his country, following his chain of command and getting the job done, but rules and regulations weren't for a man like him. The clusterfuck they'd found themselves during that last op left a bad taste in his mouth. Naming his security company after his codename was a big 'fuck you' to Uncle Sam. He'd take their money and complete missions they'd never sanction. Shadow Security was a front for the real work he did. The Shadow Ops Team completed missions the government couldn't—off the books, under the radar, no questions asked. He made the rules. Jett no longer had to follow military protocol and listen to the assholes in Washington. There was no chain of command. He'd get the damn job done his way.

"Good to see you, too, asshole," Jett said with a smirk, holding out a hand.

Gray shook it and sunk down onto a barstool beside him. His tattooed arms showed in his tee shirt, and his beard was longer than the stubble he'd had the last time Jett had seen him. "This place is a bit fancy for my blood. Have you gone soft on us?"

"I have another meeting here," Jett said with a smirk. "They picked the place. When I heard you were in town, it seemed too damn perfect. Nothing like two old Army buddies catching up."

Gray ordered a beer on tap, watching two women in tight skirts walk by. They'd ditched their suit jackets somewhere and clutched designer purses in their hands, tottering by on sky-high heels.

"Lesbians," Jett said knowingly.

Gray elbowed him. "Like hell. They were just eye-fucking the bartender."

"I'm just messing with you," Jett said with a low

chuckle. "They're probably too uptight for me," he said, letting his gaze flicker down their legs anyway. He would've chased after them for sure in his younger days. It had been years since he'd had a one-night stand. Dating? He sometimes did that. He'd see a woman occasionally, buy her something pretty, and enjoy some weekends away together. He was a man who appreciated his privacy. He managed being single just fine. It suited him, actually. He'd deployed all the time during his years of service and traveled on black ops missions now—or ran them stateside. Both required constant vigilance. How could he explain his sudden disappearances or long hours at Shadow Security with a girlfriend or wife at home?

He couldn't. Not without putting them in danger. The truth was, he'd never met a woman who was worth the trouble. Most of the women he met wouldn't appreciate a home upstate anyway, away from the hustle and bustle of city life. Never mind that his secluded home had every modern luxury, and he had a state-of-the-art facility nearby to conduct ops and training. They didn't need to know the details of how he ran Shadow Security—or what its true mission was.

Life was simpler without a woman. He was too set in his ways now anyway.

"So, what's the deal?" Gray asked, taking a sip from the pilsner glass the bartender set down in front of him. "You in some sort of trouble? Your message said it was urgent."

Jett laughed. "Hell no. I'm not in trouble."

"What was with the urgency then?" Gray said, looking pissed off. "I know you didn't want to meet up just to shoot the shit."

4

"It was urgent to me, yes. I need another guy on my team."

"Fuck no. Those days are over for me. Long over. I did my duty and have the goddamn scars to prove it."

Jett frowned, watching his former teammate. Gray had been a POW during their last op together—beaten. Tortured. They'd gotten him back after three days, but the man still bore the marks. Physical and mental scars. He also had the skills Jett needed. He was both strong and smart. Calculating. The military had known it. They all did. Now Jett just needed him back in the game. "We need a sixth guy," Jett said. "I'm running things stateside a majority of the time, but some missions require a full team. I don't like sending a man in alone. We work in pairs."

"So fucking hire someone."

"I did. He got caught in a damn honey pot."

Gray scowled, running a hand over his beard. "So find someone who doesn't think with his dick every minute of the day. There are men out there who can withstand temptation."

Jett looked at him pointedly.

"Hell no. Not me. Just because I wouldn't be whipping out my dick for the first beautiful woman who batted her eyelashes at me doesn't mean I'm the guy for the job."

"It's only part of the reason. Yes, you're too smart for that shit, but it's more. We work well together. You know that," Jett said in a low voice. "Sam, Ford, Nick, and Luke are good operatives. The best. Not everyone has that type of training and background. The new guy didn't fit in anyway. We can all practically read each other's minds. I want you in on

5

this, Gray. Think of the fucking lives you'll be saving. When the Government can't go in, we do."

"Jesus," he muttered.

Jett pulled a Shadow Security business card from his wallet. "Call the number on here. They'll help you get set up and moved to New York."

Gray eyed him warily. "You're assuming I'll take the job."

"I know you will. You think you'll be happy hanging around in pool halls all day for the rest of your life? Hell no. I need you in on this." He took the last swig of his whiskey and eyed his watch. "I've got to meet another contact in twenty minutes. He's got some papers for me."

Jett pulled his wallet out, dropping a fifty down on the bar. Fucking Manhattan.

"You're a busy man, boss."

Jett smirked. "I knew you'd be in. The others were placing bets on how long it'd take me to convince you. Fortunately, I won." He stood up from the barstool, slapping Gray on the back. "It'll be like old times, only the pay is much better. Talk to you soon."

Chapter 2

Anna Dubois cursed at the message on her cell phone, grumbling under her breath. Twelve hours in the office was enough for today, thank you very much. She needed some food for sustenance and a stiff drink—not necessarily in that order. She absolutely wasn't about to send over the updated reports a third time because her boss accidentally deleted her earlier two emails. It's like he was intentionally being an ass.

Two men in business suits nodded at her as she hurried out of the office building, her heels clacking on the floor, but she brushed past them. One of the men called out something in greeting, but she ignored him. That was also the last thing she needed—another suit in her life. Sure, he'd probably love to buy her a drink and take her back to his place, but she'd been there and done that. Her ex had been married to his career. The sex had been decent—

when they were actually having it. He was more worried about climbing the corporate ladder than her. Any man who'd take a call while in the throes of passion was not the man for her anyway. It wasn't like he'd needed to answer the phone because someone's life was in danger. He was just another Wall Street jackass. Thank God she'd never married the prick.

Anna might have a killer career as an executive assistant to a Wall Street bigwig, but damn. She liked to let loose and have fun, too. There was more to life than the office, her laptop, and late nights slaving away over financial reports. She'd once thought she wanted to be a broker herself, but no way. Life was too short to be stuck here in New York City forever. Maybe she should jet off to Hollywood and find herself a movie star. Not.

None of the men she'd met recently appealed to her—no doubt because they were all the damn same. A man in a fancy suit more concerned about his portfolio and designer clothes didn't really spark any intrigue. There were hundreds of other guys just like that within spitting distance.

She tugged her blonde strands free from the prim and proper bun she'd worn to meetings all day, letting it fall down her back. She tousled it a bit as she walked toward the closest bar, ignoring the looks of a cabbie waiting for his customer to climb in. Her friends were meeting uptown tonight, but she didn't want to sit in traffic for an hour to get there. Anna's nerves were shot, and if she didn't start downing drinks, she was going to lose it. This damn city was too much sometimes.

Her phone buzzed with another text, and she resisted the urge to scream in frustration.

Pausing on the busy sidewalk, she forwarded her boss the same email for the third time and then quickly sent her best friend Ashleigh a text.

Anna: *Sorry I can't make it. Just left the office, and my brain is fried.*

Her gaze flicked toward the skyscraper she'd just exited. Funny how what was so shiny and enticing a few years ago now just felt like a damn prison. Arriving before seven to appease her boss's insane demands and then staying a full twelve hours every day was wearing on her. Her entire body was simply exhausted, and she was looking forward to sitting down on a barstool and ignoring all the demands of her life for the evening.

Her phone buzzed, and she glanced down at Ashleigh's text.

Ashleigh: *What? Get your booty up here, hun. Jen and I are waiting.*

Anna smiled.

Anna: *My dancing on bar days have been over since college. You know that.*

Anna: *Don't do anything I wouldn't do. xoxo*

Her phone buzzed again, but she was already crossing with the light, cabs honking at the slow pedestrians. Jesus. She'd lived in Manhattan since graduating college five years ago. At first, she loved the hustle and bustle of life in the Big Apple, but more often than not, now it grated on her nerves. She needed to jet off to a tropical resort for a week or two—maybe even just a quick escape upstate to the mountains. She wasn't exactly an outdoorsy girl, but she could chill with wine in a cabin or something. Didn't people do that? Go to their upstate properties on lakes or whatever? A hot tub in a secluded mountain retreat sounded pretty damn fantastic. Returning to her own cramped Manhattan studio was not exactly appealing. Life in New York might've been exciting, but when you were too damn busy to enjoy it, what was the point?

Ashleigh had a cute little studio in Brooklyn and was a romance novelist. Her books were already beginning to take off, and Anna had no doubt she was at the beginning of an amazing career as an author. Ashleigh was already saving up for her own two-bedroom place. She'd probably find a guy, get married, and be living the dream soon.

As for Anna's own life? She'd loved the stockbroker type when she'd first arrived in the city, but those guys were all the same. They were focused on money, booze, and getting the most gorgeous woman into their bed. It was exciting until it wasn't. She was never home, so who cared where she lived. She didn't even get to enjoy her tiny, cramped place.

Her boss would no doubt love to sleep with her, but gross. The guy was in his fifties, old enough to be her father. He'd probably put her up in a penthouse somewhere as his mistress since she didn't think his divorce was ever finalized, but hell no to that. She needed to start looking for a new job if she didn't want to deal with his advances anymore. If only she had the time to do it.

Pulling open the door to the bar down the block, she let the conversation and music dull her thoughts. Anna just needed a few drinks to unwind. And some damn food.

A couple kissing at the bar moved away, and she quickly slid onto the barstool, gesturing to the bartender. She crossed her legs, the skirt of her suit riding higher on her thighs. Her feet were killing her after walking around in heels all day, but she couldn't be bothered to switch into flats like some women preferred. Anna ordered a gin and tonic, taking a careful sip. Hell. She really wanted a couple shots of whiskey.

Her gaze flicked around the crowded bar. Most people were dressed in business suits like her. It wasn't exactly surprising given they were in the financial district. She saw a woman from her office flirting with a stockbroker she recognized. Stiffening slightly, her eyes moved around the bar again. She didn't mind seeing her colleagues as long as her boss wasn't here. Had he gotten her third email?

Ugh.

Pulling out her phone, she quickly swiped the screen. No news was good news, so she shoved it back into her bag. He'd just have to deal without the report if he deleted her third email.

A rowdy group of youngish guys at the end of the bar were knocking back drinks, and a few women nearby were eying them. She'd done exactly the same a few short years ago. Funny how jaded she already felt. She was twenty-seven, not fifty. She took another sip of her drink, trying to relax, when her eyes landed on a gruffly handsome man seated across the bar from her. He'd been watching the crowd, but when his dark gaze landed on her, she felt pinned in place by his stare. Dark stubble covered his jaw, and his hair was cropped short. He looked older than her by probably a decade. Maybe more. His cool confidence was evident all the way across the room. This was a guy comfortable in his own skin. She definitely didn't get the Wall Street vibe from him. He was far too muscular to sit at a desk all day.

Anna felt butterflies fill her stomach as she took in his broad shoulders and thick arms.

Damn.

Even his hands were sexy. He was gripping a beer bottle, the veins standing out. And his forearms—hell. She had a vision of those arms beside her head on the mattress as he caged her in, ducking down to kiss her thoroughly.

There was no thousand-dollar suit on this guy. He had on a polo shirt, but it looked lived-in. Not worn out—just the type of clothes a man really wore. He was practical, not trying to impress the crowd with designer clothes or expensive drinks. Still, he had the confidence of a man with money and power. He just didn't need to show it off.

He was still looking at her, and she swore her girly parts clenched.

It had been a long time since she'd had good sex. Too long. Her ex hadn't been too impressive in bed, and there'd been that one drunken weekend with another man at least a year ago. He was visiting New York, and she'd known it was just a fling. They'd had a fun twelve hours, and then she'd sent him on his way. He was from South Carolina, and she knew she'd never see him again. Anna didn't have time to date. She was no longer attracted to the type of men she worked with. And she couldn't stop staring at this ruggedly handsome man.

Holy crap, he was standing up.

She sipped her drink again as he moved toward her. It was like a goddamn scene from a movie. She couldn't have avoided his heated gaze if she wanted. One moment he'd been watching her, and the next, he was crossing the bar, getting closer with each heartbeat. She downed the rest of her gin and tonic, and he eyed her empty glass as he stopped next to her barstool. "Can I buy you another one?" His voice was deep. Smooth. And the male interest in his eyes had all of her taking notice.

"No. I wouldn't turn down a shot of whiskey though."

A smile tugged on the corner of his lips. He gestured to the bartender and ordered them each a shot before sinking down onto the barstool beside her. His gaze trailed over her, causing her heart to flutter. She was in a suit, not sexy dress, but his appreciative gaze made her blood warm. Her breasts pressed against the thin camisole she had on beneath her blazer. Her skirt showed off her toned legs. She was thankful she still had on her heels, not frumpy flats. Her feet were killing her, but damn. At least she looked good.

"Do you work around here?" he asked.

The bartender slid two shots toward them, and Anna picked one up, smiling at the handsome stranger. "That I do. And thank God it's Friday. Cheers."

"I'll drink to that," he said with a low chuckle. He downed the shot at the same time as her, and the whiskey burned down her throat. She heard her phone buzzing in her purse, but she ignored it. Her boss was probably on her ass again about those damn financial reports she'd already sent. Three times. Anna was off the clock as far as she was concerned.

"Just my boss again. I've had twelve-hour days all week and don't need him riding my ass." She practically snorted. "I mean, he'd love that, right?

Like I'm the type to sleep with my boss. Besides. He's old enough to be my father."

"He's sexually harassing you."

"He's a dick. All the women in the office steer clear." Her gaze flicked over him. "Do you work around here? I'm not getting the stockbroker vibe."

He shook his head, those full lips slightly quirking. "No. I had several meetings in the city today. I live upstate." That might explain the more casual clothes that he was wearing. She wondered what type of meetings he'd been attending. Certainly not any on Wall Street.

"I'm Anna," she said, holding out one perfectly manicured hand.

"Jett." His thick fingers closed around hers, sending electricity shooting straight through her. His hand was warm. Solid. Rough. He smelled of pine trees and forest. The way he looked like he wanted to eat her right up probably should have frightened her, but after the suits she dealt with all the time? She inexplicably felt safe with him. That was probably foolish. She didn't know this guy from a random stranger on the street. There was no logical reason to feel safe with him.

His gaze shifted as a loud conversation erupted across the bar, and then his focus was once again on her.

"You're not a cop, are you?" she asked quizzically.

"No. Why? Have you done something illegal?"

She burst into laughter. "No. You just seem intense. Aware of your surroundings. If you told me you worked at a desk all day, I'd never believe it."

"I'm former military, and I run my own security business now."

"Oh," she said, surprised. She didn't get the business owner vibe from this man, whatever that was. She could see the military connection though. It explained why he was muscular in a way the men who lifted at the gym never would be. There was a slight roughness to Jett, an edge that the men she worked with never would have. "And you had meetings here for work?"

"I met up with an old buddy of mine for a drink. I also had a client who needed help tracking someone down. I came into the city to meet with him and see what we could do."

"So what, you're like a bounty hunter?" she teased.

"Sort of, sweetness," he said with that slow smile that made her insides churn. Damn. This guy was so smooth, he could probably just look at a woman and have her hop into bed with him. She raised her eyebrows.

"What?" he asked, his full lips quirking in amusement. "I bet you're sweet all over."

"Wouldn't you love to find out."

"You'll get no arguments from me," he said with a low chuckle. Jett ordered another round of shots. She'd probably be offended if some slick Wall Street shark said that to her. Jett was a complete one-eighty from the men she knew. He was raw and real. Masculine. She could sense the power underneath that cool exterior. He shifted slightly, his muscled arm brushing against her. He was probably around six-feet tall. In her heels, he only had a few inches on her.

Anna slipped off her blazer, draping it neatly across her lap. Her camisole hugged her full breasts, and she saw Jett's gaze briefly dart there before he smiled at her again. "What are you doing here alone tonight, Anna? I assume a beautiful woman like you who works here in the city would have friends or a boyfriend to go out with on a Friday night."

"Yes to the friends, no to the boyfriend. And truth be told, I was supposed to meet up with some girlfriends. It would take me an hour to head uptown though, and I needed a drink after my day."

"A drink before drinks," he said with a low chuckle. "Fair enough." He looked amused as he watched her, those dark eyes not missing a thing. "Are you meeting with them later?"

"Probably not." A beat passed, almost as if the possibilities of the night were unfolding before them. "What about you? You wanted a night in the city before heading back home? What happened to the old friend you met up with?"

"Ah. He found a date for the evening," Jett said with a grin. "Who am I to get between a man and his love life?"

"So, no cock blocking from you."

Jett burst into laughter, the deep rumble sending shivers through her body. He scrubbed a hand over the stubble on his jaw. "Negative. I understand how the bro code works. I'll head back upstate after the city traffic dies down a bit. My client let me park at his building, so there's no rush. No doubt the parking would otherwise be astronomical here. I'm not big on public transportation."

"You like to be in control," she surmised. "I can see that. And I hear you on Manhattan. I've got the tiniest studio imaginable yet pay a small fortune. An actual house upstate sounds heavenly."

The bartender slid their shots across the bar, and Anna picked hers up. Jett clinked his glass against hers. "Cheers." He downed it in one gulp again as Anna took a sip of hers. She still hadn't eaten yet, but after the whiskey burned down her throat, she finished the rest of her shot. The slight buzz was making her more daring than usual—not that she was exactly some shrinking violet. Still, if Jett bought her another drink, she'd have to decline or at least order some food.

"This is nice, but I enjoy sipping whiskey on my back porch," Jett said, holding his empty shot glass. His muscular fingers turned the glass, and she had the random thought of those hands gliding over her body. His self-assured behavior and confidence were intriguing. He wasn't pushy but clearly knew his likes and dislikes.

And he was obviously interested in her.

"It's bound to be more peaceful than here. My parents used to live in Connecticut, so I'd escape the city when I could for a weekend."

"Good for you. I don't think I'm cut out for city life."

Anna laughed. "Me either, but here I am."

He smiled again, his eyes comfortably resting on her. In a weird way, it felt like she'd known him for years. Anna was far more comfortable with this stranger than any of the men she'd dated since moving to New York City. He was confident but not outwardly trying to impress her, bragging about his portfolio or trust fund. He owned his own security company for goodness's sake. Clearly, he must have some success if he was meeting clients here in the city. She didn't get the sense that he was lying. Anna worked with sleazy guys in suits all day long. Jett let off an entirely different aura.

"Did you move to Manhattan for work or a man?" he asked, those dark eyes focused on her.

"Work. My college roommate and I both ended up here, although she lives in Brooklyn now. She's a writer."

"And you?"

"Executive assistant. I essentially run the office at this point. It's all boring as hell, but my boss thinks everything he says is of the utmost importance." She brushed her hair back over her shoulder. "The pay is good, the hours suck, and I realized I don't love the city."

He watched her, and she could tell he was really listening. Some men would wait for her to finish speaking only to blurt out whatever they wanted to say. Jett paid attention. "You're young. You could do something else or work as an executive assistant somewhere with a better boss—one who doesn't hit on anyone in a skirt. There are plenty of companies that could use your skill set."

"Yeah, I might. Now I just need a spare hour in the day to job hunt."

"If anything, you'll be getting away from your sleazy boss. Life's too short to put up with that."

"I know. That's what my best friend said, too."

"I like her already," Jett joked. "Not in the same way that I like you though." He shifted infinitesimally closer. She could feel the heat from his body. The bar had been gradually filling up around them, but she'd been so engrossed in their conversation, she hadn't even noticed.

"How old are you?" she asked.

"Forty-two. I did a decade in the service and then eventually started my own security business after I got out."

Anna would've guessed he was younger, maybe mid-thirties or so. He was fit and attractive. Handsome. She didn't usually have much interest in men more than a few years older than her. They tended to be stuffy and boring or completely full of themselves. Jett had an aura of danger about him. The man was former military. No doubt he was positively lethal. He wouldn't hurt her though. She might be young, but she'd always had a good read on people.

"And the men who work for you, are they all former military, too?" she asked.

He nodded. She couldn't imagine what exactly he did. Jett had said he owned a security business, but she didn't think he was going around installing home surveillance systems. This guy had an intense, slightly dangerous vibe. She wasn't scared of him, but she was also smart enough to know he wasn't telling her everything. He had clients in the city. He hadn't hired regular civilians. She'd been joking when she asked if he was a bounty hunter, but now she wondered how far off that guess had really been. It was unusual to meet a random stranger in a bar and instantly hit it off, especially a man who in theory had little in common with her. That didn't stop the feelings of awareness that prickled over her at his closeness or the sense that she could trust him.

"I built up a team of men to work for my company. Most I know from my own military days."

"You can't tell me exactly what you do."

"No, sweetness. I can't." Jett's gaze landed on her empty shot glass. "Would you like another drink, Anna?"

She shook her head, her body heating as he watched her. He was an attractive man. Jett was different from men she'd dated in the past, and she was drawn to him in a way she didn't fully understand.

"Can I buy you dinner?" he asked. Those dark eyes were studying her. Careful. Watchful.

"I'm considering it," she said. "What'd you have in mind?" She shifted her legs on the barstool, her skirt hitching up slightly. Jett's gaze on her thighs shouldn't have made her pulse pound. They were just having drinks. That was all. She might've been wilder in her college days, but she worked on Wall Street now. She was an adult. She didn't sleep with men she'd just met.

But she loved the way Jett was watching her. Her eyes tracked over his features—chiseled jaw. Slight stubble. Full lips.

"What would you do if I kissed you?" he asked, his voice low.

Her breath caught as she looked at him again, her lips parting slightly. Jett was deceivingly calm, but she sensed his very real male interest in her. He wasn't leering or aggressive. He wasn't making her uncomfortable. In a way, his directness was almost refreshing. Jett knew what he wanted. He took a swig of the beer he'd carried over, his big hand clutching the bottle. His Adam's apple bobbed as he swallowed. This man was sexy without even trying. Gruff. Raw. Real.

His gaze slid to her again, waiting for an answer.

Was he always a gentleman? She assumed not. And while she could deny it all she wanted, she was dying to feel his lips on hers.

"I'd wonder what's taking you so damn long."

The air felt electric around them as Jett leaned toward her. The conversations at the bar, the music, and everything else faded into the background. His deep brown eyes locked on hers, and she felt trapped. Pinned in place by this man she barely knew. Jett palmed her cheek, his hand warm even against her heated skin. His thumb lightly brushed over her lips for the briefest of moments. His other hand landed on the back of her head, his fingers tangling in her hair as he angled her head.

It didn't feel like he wanted a simple kiss. It felt like he was staking his claim.

"Sweet Anna," he murmured. And then he ducked and was kissing her. Taking what he wanted. He tasted of whiskey and man, but he was gentle. Careful with her. His whiskers rubbed against her sensitive skin, raw and masculine. He kissed her again, slowly, taking his time to see what she liked. To learn how she responded. Anna gasped, shocked at how aroused she felt from just a kiss. When he pulled back, lazily grinning down at her, her heart nearly pounded out of her chest. He hadn't just kissed her—he'd given her a taste of what could come. His muscular hand brushed back some of her blonde hair, as if he couldn't resist touching her. "You should come home with me."

It was insane. Crazy. She shouldn't even consider it.

She could feel her heart racing even as desire pooled at her core. That kiss. She was still breathless. "How do I know you're not some ax murderer or something?"

"I'll keep you safe, Anna."

She had no reason to believe him aside from her gut instincts. He could be lying. He could be a serial killer. A drug dealer. A rapist. She wouldn't go back to the apartment of a man here in Manhattan for a one-night-stand, so why would she go with this guy?

"We can head up there tonight. You. Me. Alone. Away from the crowds of Manhattan. Unless you'd rather be in the cramped studio apartment of yours. My place is tucked away in the woods, but it's got everything you could want there." He touched her again, his hand resting on her bare forearm. The heat from his fingertips burned into her skin. He was waiting for her to decide.

"How would I get back to the city? I don't have a car."

"I'll drive you back tomorrow. Sunday if it goes well," he added with an easy grin.

Heat blossomed over her skin. "I don't have a change of clothes with me. Won't that be a problem?"

Those thick fingers caressed her arm again. "I've got extra, but I'm not planning for us to need much in the way of clothing. My hot tub is out on the back deck and private. I live alone. It'll just be you and me, sweetness. You can wear my clothes or nothing at all. I'm sure you can guess my preference."

"Let me see your driver's license."

His lips quirked, but he dutifully pulled out his wallet, handing his license over to her. "I'm going to text a picture of this to my friends. And my parents. Maybe one of my coworkers, too," she added.

He nodded, not objecting to any of that. "That's smart. Go ahead. Whatever makes you feel comfortable. Here, I'll give you a business card, too."

She looked at him doubtfully. "You don't care if I send them all your information?"

"I want you to feel safe. I want you to come with me, too. If coming to my place means you tell everyone you know my name, then so be it. I don't have anything to hide."

Eyeing him warily, she took a picture of his license and texted it to Ashleigh and Jen. They'd wonder what the heck was going on, but she didn't care. She was tired of New York and her crazy job and obnoxious boss. He'd probably be texting her again tomorrow morning, asking for some damn report. Jett was the first real thing that had happened to her since moving here. That single kiss made her feel more alive than any of the nights in bed with her ex. And getting out of the city for a night? Going someplace where she could actually breathe and not be surrounded by people? That sounded great, too.

Their fingers brushed as she handed him back his driver's license, sending sparks shooting right through her. She'd quickly calculated his age—forty-two, just like he'd said. Fifteen years older than her. Anna's eyes landed again on the sexy man in front of her. He was sinfully dangerous. Probably lethal, too, around the right people. Or was that the wrong people? She didn't have a problem with him fighting the bad guys. Still, this was impulsive, even for her.

She knew she'd regret it forever if she said no.

"So is that a yes, sweetheart? Get out of here with me?"

"Kiss me again first," she demanded.

He chuckled but shifted closer, cupping her face as he leaned in. Jett brushed a feather light kiss over her mouth, shockingly sensual. She could already tell he'd be an attentive lover. She'd never felt so turned on in her life, and all they'd done was kiss right here in the crowded bar.

Jett's lips moved to her ear. "I'll kiss you all over when we get to my place," he murmured.

"Yes," she said breathlessly. "Let's get out of here."

Jett peeled a couple of twenties out of his wallet and laid them down on the bar to cover their drinks. He held out an arm, allowing her to step down from her barstool. Anna's eyes slid to his. "Are we going to dinner or your house?"

"Dinner first, sweetness. I'm starving. But I already know what I'm having for dessert," he added with a wink.

Chapter 3

Jett led Anna out of the bar, his arm wrapping around her slender waist. It was instinctual, wanting to hold her close. She was several inches shorter than him in those sexy heels, and he couldn't wait to see her in them and nothing else later on. She was young. Beautiful. Burned out already from the hustle and bustle of New York. Part of him wanted to sweep her off her feet and never let her go. He didn't even want to consider where that thought had come from. He'd never needed a woman before. What made her so different?

She leaned into him ever-so-slightly, causing the edge of his lips to quirk. That kiss had been intimate, considering they were in the middle of a crowd of people. Without even realizing it, Anna had submitted to him. Let him take the lead. He didn't miss how aroused she was at his touch. Her nipples had pebbled against her camisole. She'd gasped as his lips moved over hers. Jett couldn't wait to taste her everywhere.

It was insane how much his body craved her. When was the last time he'd picked up a woman at a bar? Years ago. And as attracted as he was to Anna, he also enjoyed talking with her. It made no sense. She knew nothing about the military or the types of missions he ran. She didn't run in the same social circles as him. She was so far removed from his world it was almost funny.

That didn't stop the way his blood heated when she was near. He loved her sense of humor and laugh. Her wit and charm. Her boss sounded like a dick, from the little she'd told him. He was half-tempted to offer her a job himself, but he didn't mix business with pleasure. And he very much wanted the pleasure of her company.

"Thanks for the drinks," she said as they walked out into the evening. He'd been in that bar for hours, but the highlight of his day had been when Anna walked in. She hadn't noticed him at first. He'd watched her turn down other men as she confidently strode right up to an empty barstool.

She was tempting as hell but smart. Sharp. She also made him feel lighter than he had in years. Was he really bringing a woman he'd just met to his home? Sure, he'd done shit like that when he was younger, but even then, it had been different. A barely furnished apartment during his military days wasn't the same as inviting a woman he'd just met into his home. His sanctuary. He couldn't tell her anything about Shadow Security—nothing more than the cover story at any rate. But she'd see his photos and belongings. Piece together his adventurous life.

Jett had spent a decade in the Army, serving on Delta Force. His unit dealt with counterterrorism, hostage rescue, and reconnaissance missions. His own brother was also in Special Forces, albeit serving as a Navy SEAL. They'd been competitive growing up, despite Jett being the older of the two. Now Slate commanded several SEAL teams in Coronado. Jett was clear across the country from him, leading his own missions—just not under the military chain of command's watchful eye. Slate was always more of the rule follower between the two brothers. Jett enjoyed being the wildcard. It had served him well over the years. He did what he damn well pleased and apologized later. You wouldn't get anything in life by sitting back and watching the world pass by.

"Where do you want to eat?" Anna asked, looking up at him.

She hadn't pulled away when he'd snared his arm around her, and Jett loved that. Her suit jacket was draped over one of her arms, along with her purse, and he got an eyeful of sexy cleavage. Anna wore a few long, gold necklaces that dangled enticingly between her breasts. Her earrings shimmered as she moved. She wore several rings as well. She was feminine and sexy. When she shifted slighter closer to him, Jett noticed that she inexplicably smelled like peaches and cream. He'd almost expected something bolder. Stronger. She really was sweet all over.

"There's a great steakhouse nearby. I meet with clients there, so they know me. We'll have no problems getting a table. What do you say?"

"Sounds heavenly," she admitted. "I skipped lunch because I was so busy today."

Jett frowned. Anna was svelte and sexy, but she

needed to eat. "You need a break, and you shouldn't skip meals.

She shrugged, her breasts moving with the gesture. "Yeah, well, tell that to my boss. I end up redoing the same stuff again and again because he's a moron. He already texted several times after I left the office."

"I wouldn't mind a word with him," Jett muttered.

"Are you sure we can get in to this place? It looks crowded," she said as they stopped walking in front of an expensive steakhouse.

He lightly squeezed her waist. "They know me. My team has meetings here a lot."

"In the financial district?" she asked doubtfully.

"Whatever works," he said with a smile. "My clients are happy with whatever I suggest. We do switch it up occasionally, but what can I say? I like what I like."

"You have meetings here for all the security work you do."

"Affirmative. You spend enough money somewhere, and they're happy to accommodate. We'll get in. The food is fantastic, and they've got a great wine list. We'll have dinner, drinks, and then head out of the city. The traffic should've mostly died down by then. I'm thinking a night in my hot tub looking out at the stars sounds—"

"Heavenly," Anna interrupted.

His lips quirked. "You took the words right out of my mouth." Unable to resist, he leaned in and kissed her temple. That fucking peaches and cream. Would she taste like that all over? Was her skin this satiny soft everywhere? Jett was dying to find out.

***

Two hours later, Anna was riding in the passenger seat of Jett's large black SUV. The lights of New York City twinkled behind them, and as he drove through the night, Jett was trying to remember the last time he felt so alive. "God. I can't believe we're doing this," she said with a giggle, looking over at him with a smile. "I never do anything like this, just so you know. Not to say I haven't had a one-night-stand before, but no. Not anymore. I've left those days behind me and am a responsible, upstanding citizen now."

His lips quirked as she rambled on. "And I wouldn't go home with just anyone you know."

"I'm glad you made an exception for me," he said dryly.

They'd shared a bottle of expensive red wine over dinner, eaten salad and steaks, and enjoyed snuggling up together in a private booth. Aside from a few stolen kisses, nothing inappropriate had happened. Jett was a gentleman. He wasn't about to paw at a woman in the middle of a restaurant. The conversation had flowed as easily as the wine, surprising him. It wasn't often he met a woman he wanted to spend more time with and actually get to know. Anna might be younger than him, but she wasn't naïve. Living in Manhattan would toughen up anyone, he supposed.

"You're different from other men I know."

He smirked. It was just a coincidence that he'd literally been thinking she was different from other women. "I'm no suit on Wall Street. I saw you as soon as you walked into the bar earlier," he admitted.

"Hmmm. So, you were waiting to make a move?"

"Something like that. And Anna?" He looked over at her for a beat. "I don't do things like this either. I'm busy with work. Running my security company takes up most of my time. I don't date."

"Don't worry. I'm not expecting to fly you to Florida to meet my parents next weekend. Actually, they'd love you though. Ironic, right? My last boyfriend was always on his phone watching the stock market, following financial advice. They thought he was all wrong for me and out of touch with the rest of the world."

He raised an eyebrow. "Were they right?"

She shrugged. "Yeah. They were. He didn't seem to know life existed outside of Manhattan. And trust me, I hate admitting that my parents were right about anything."

He chuckled, then reached over and took her hand. "Well, I told you I never date because I don't want you to think I do this all the time either. I'm attracted to you, but there's something else here, too. I don't spend hours talking with every beautiful woman I meet."

She looked up at him, smiling again. Was this woman ever unhappy? She'd claimed to dislike her boss and career, but she'd been flirty and fun the several hours they'd been together. "There is something here, isn't there? I wouldn't say it's love at first sight, because I don't believe in that sort of thing. But if I did? Yeah. Absolutely. That's what this is."

His thumb ran over her smooth skin. She was right that love at first sight didn't exist. He wasn't sure he believed in love anyway. Not for him at any rate. Lust? That he was familiar with. Not that he acted much on those urges either. He was old enough to know what he wanted in life. The spark between Anna and him was something new. He wanted her, but he also wanted to get to know her. She made him laugh. Smile. Jett, a hardened former Delta who led a black ops team. An unfamiliar feeling wound through him. He wanted to protect Anna in a way that didn't make sense.

"Maybe it's kismet," he joked. "We can try to avoid falling in love all we want, but it's fate. It'll happen." He glanced over at her and winked. Another thing he didn't usually do. Something about Anna made him want to put her at ease. Make her feel safe with him.

"Huh. You believe in that sort of thing?"

"I believe anything's possible," he admitted in a low voice. "I've seen the worst of the world at times. I spent years in the military, traveling to all sorts of godforsaken places. I've seen men who were beaten and killed. Children who were slaughtered. I've seen amazing things happen, too."

She shivered slightly at his side.

"Sorry. I didn't mean to bring up such a depressing topic." He gently squeezed her hand.

"You can talk to me," she assured him. "I might not get all of it, being that's not my area of expertise, but I'm a good listener."

"You are," he agreed. "I'm not sure this is typical first date talk though." Anna had listened to some of his military stories over dinner and a bottle of wine. He'd asked about her job as well. They were as different as could be as far as their careers went. He couldn't deny the way he was inexplicably drawn to her though. He didn't want to let her out of his sight. "I told you that I'm forty-two. How about you, sweetness? I know it's not polite to ask a woman her age—"

"But you're no gentleman," she joked.

Jett burst into laughter. "What gave you that idea?" He glanced over to see her smirk. Hell. Even her sass was adorable.

"I'm twenty-seven. Old enough to have settled down, according to my mother. I told her no one marries that young in New York. We've got careers and exciting single lives to lead."

"And do you?"

"Goodness, no. I'm stuck at my desk all day. I do go out with friends, but it's not all that I thought it would be. Yes, it was fun for a while, but how many years can I do the same thing? I don't know. Maybe I'm just ready for a change." Her phone buzzed, and Jett watched her pull it from her purse. "Speaking of my friends, they're just making sure I'm still alive. I'll quick shoot them a text back."

"Let me talk to them," Jett said.

"Oh yes, good idea," she agreed. "I'm convinced they half thought I was joking that I was going home with you. Sending a photo of your license was a nice touch." Anna pushed the call button, and they heard the phone ringing. Nope. Definitely not what one normally did with their one-night-stand.

"Hi! Are you okay?" a female voice asked. "Are you alive? I looked up this guy to make sure he's legit."

"You're on speaker phone!" Anna trilled. "And he's right here with me. Is Jen there, too?"

"Anna!" her friend protested. "Why didn't you say I was on speaker?"

"I literally just did! What are you talking about?

Pay attention. We're in the car heading out of the city. Jett and I had dinner, and now we're heading back to his place."

Jett shook his head, trying to resist the urge to smile. He heard her friend mumble something. "Yes, we're both here."

"Hello ladies," he said smoothly.

"You're Jett?" a new voice asked suspiciously.

"I am. To whom am I speaking?"

"That was Jen. Ashleigh was the uptight one who answered," Anna said.

"Good grief," Jen, the second woman, said. "We're her best friends. You better bring her back in one piece. Anna, call us if you need anything. Anything! I know people," she warned him.

"I'm glad Anna has such protective friends," he assured the women. "I promise you that she's in good hands with me. If she wants to come home for any reason, I'll bring her right back to the city. Door to door service. Promise."

"I looked up your company," Ashleigh said. "We'll leave you bad reviews all over the Internet if you hurt Anna."

"Fair enough," he said easily. "I'm not going to hurt her," he added in a low voice.

"Guys, you're embarrassing me!" Anna wailed. She winked at Jett, and he had to hold back his laughter. This woman.

"Sorry," both of the women said.

"Seriously, call us if you need something," one of them said.

"I'll have Anna check in with you tomorrow," Jett told them. "Would that work?"

"Yes, that would work," Ashleigh agreed.

"Otherwise, we'll track you down."

"Understood."

"Bye girls!" Anna said, ending the call. She looked over at Jett, a huge smile on her face. "That was pretty funny but not actually a bad idea. I didn't really send your license to my parents and coworkers, in case you were wondering."

"You could've."

She shrugged, leaning back into his passenger seat. "I know, but there was no need." She'd put her blazer back on as the night had cooled off, and he was looking very much forward to peeling it off her later. Anna was a knockout—flirty and fun. Witty. Really, the total package. He liked that she was younger than him. Maybe that made him a caveman, but Jett rather liked the idea of taking care of her.

And as for tonight? They had less than an hour until they were home. He had some whiskey, a hot tub, and the gorgeous night with a beautiful woman to enjoy.

Chapter 4

"Oh my God, this is beautiful," Anna said as they pulled up his long driveway. His home was set back from the winding road, and the gate clanked shut behind them as he pulled through. Lighting lit the property, showcasing his home. Shadow Security had even tighter measures in place to ensure no one accessed the property—fingerprint scanners, gates and keyed entryways. His own home was set back from the main road and had cameras, fences, and alarms. Not to mention a wide expanse of woods surrounding it, ensuring not just anyone could show up at the door. No one would breach the property without his knowledge.

"You didn't tell me you lived in a mansion," Anna continued.

Jett chuckled, clicking the door to his three-car garage. "It's not exactly a mansion."

"Compared to my studio apartment? Oh, it is. No

wonder you couldn't wait to escape the city and come up here. It's like heaven on earth."

He glanced over at her in amusement, pulling into his garage. His motorcycle was off to one side, along with a smaller sports car. "Did I mention my home is on the lake?"

"What? No, you did not. It's cold this time of year, right? I didn't even bring a swimsuit."

He shut off the engine, smiling. "Well, there's something to be said for skinny dipping. It is too cold now though. My hot tub is out back in the patio area. It's perfect for nights like this."

"It sounds incredible. Oh my God, you have to show me around."

"I'll get your door." He strode around his SUV, helping Anna to step out. Jett had to blink in surprise as he took her hand in his own. The rightness of her here in his garage, getting out of his vehicle, was astounding. He'd never even wanted to bring a woman back here before, but Anna? It was like she just fit. This was just a weekend adventure though. They'd enjoy a night or two together, and he'd have to get her back to the city.

"You must be a night owl like me," she said, looking up at him.

"Guilty as charged. I tend to rise fairly early as well. I don't need much sleep."

"Lucky you. I'd love to sleep in if I could. I can never manage to get to bed early on the weekends."

"Well, if I wake you up tomorrow, I promise it'll be worth your while," he said, a smile tugging at his lips. "But us night owls all know the best things happen after midnight."

"I thought nothing good happens after midnight,"

she teased, letting him hold her hand and guide her inside. Jett entered the alarm code, flipping on another light as he let her into his home.

"What can I get you?" he asked. She was looking around, taking in every detail. He'd hired a decorator since he didn't have the first clue about such things. He had an entire support staff at Shadow Security. He arranged the missions, but they kept things running. His household would be hopeless without his staff as well. As he'd told Anna, he lived alone. They came during the week or as needed.

"Water to start with," she said, studying some pictures on the wall. "Do you have a brother?"

Jett's gaze landed on the picture. "Yes. Slate's a Navy SEAL commander stationed on the West Coast."

She made a face. "A Navy officer? He's probably strait-laced and boring."

Jeff chuckled. "You hit the nail on the head. We're opposites in many ways. But I was former military, too. I just didn't want to make a lifetime career out of it."

"You didn't get kicked out, did you?" she asked, her eyes meeting his.

"Negative, sweetness. I just prefer calling the shots. Owning my own company grants me that. I'll get you a glass of water. And whiskey afterward?"

She licked her lips but looked back to his wall of photographs. "Sounds perfect."

Jett crossed over to her, wrapping his arms around her waist and pulling her close. Anna had already set her purse down and shucked off her blazer. She still wore her come-fuck-me heels. Hell. How she could be both sexy and intriguing was a curiosity. Some beautiful women relied only on their looks. She was both charming and intelligent.

"You look good in my house," he murmured, softly kissing her temple.

Her gaze met his in the hallway mirror. "You look good wrapped around me."

"This is where I should say something crass, like how I'd look good inside of you." He kissed her temple again, inhaling her sweet scent.

She gently nudged back against him, her ass brushing against his stiffening cock. "I'm sure you would."

"Come on," he said, pulling back but letting one hand briefly rest on her backside as he guided her down the hall. His blood was heating from her nearness, his erection already straining against his pants. "Drinks and then I'll show you around." She strode in front of him, her hips swaying back and forth. Blonde hair glimmered down over her camisole. Jett wanted to stretch her out and explore every inch of her. Make her forget about everything but him.

He adjusted his aching cock as she stopped in the kitchen, admiring the sleek stainless steel. He was going to be hard all night around her, but Jett didn't want to rush things. He had a feeling she was the type of woman who'd always have him on his toes—and always have his dick standing up and paying attention.

He filled two glasses with ice water as she looked around. "Do you like to cook?" Anna asked.

"I make a few specialty dishes—mostly out of necessity. I had to learn how to cook somewhere along the line. Now I have someone come in during the week and prepare a few meals. Some nights I'm working late and eat at the office with my team." He crossed to the cabinet, pulling out a bottle of whiskey. "How about you? Do you like cooking?"

"I don't mind it. The kitchen at my place sucks—no counter space and barely an oven. I make do, but…." She shrugged. Jett poured them each two fingers of whiskey. Anna had already crossed the kitchen. He handed her the glass of whiskey, trying to ignore the sparks between them as her slender fingers brushed against his. Jett needed to show her around, to let her feel comfortable here in his space.

Anna had other ideas though. "Is this the way to the patio?"

She strode through his kitchen like she owned the place, Jett lingering behind her as he enjoyed the view. That ass in her skirt. She'd be the death of him. His hand landed on the back of her neck as she paused at the door. His thumb swept over her delicate skin. "Let me unlock it, Anna. There's an alarm set."

She looked up at him, lips parting, and Jett ducked down slowly. Their mouths met, and Anna nipped at him, Jett growling. He unlocked the door with one hand, still kissing her, and guided her out to his back patio. The night sky shone through the trees, and he flicked a switch, the hot tub bubbling to life. Dim light filled the back patio, and Anna was taking a sip of her whiskey, a smile on her lips.

"I'd never leave if I lived here. It's amazing."

Jett set his own drink down and stalked closer. "I'd never leave if you were here either."

"Awww. That's sweet."

"Are you going to join me in the hot tub?"

She smiled seductively, setting her own glass on a table, then reached down to lift her camisole up and over her head. Jett stilled. Anna in her lacy bra and tight skirt was a sight to behold. She still had her heels on, elongating those sexy legs. She turned slightly, unzipping the back of her skirt. A moment later, it fell to the ground, revealing her sexy black panties. Jett swallowed. "I don't know," Anna pondered. "Should I get in like this?" She twirled in a circle, seeming to enjoy Jett watching her. Her hands moved to her bra clasp, and then it too fell away, showing him her perfect, creamy breasts.

Jett growled and moved toward her. One hand palmed the back of her head, and Jett kissed her as he cupped one breast. She was full. Soft. His thumb skated over her nipple. "Anna. You're too damn tempting." He kissed her again, deeper, backing her toward one of his lounge chairs. She had on nothing but panties and heels, and he had to touch her before he exploded. The hot tub and whiskey could wait. He was about to drive her wild with desire.

"No hot tub?" she teased as she broke their kiss, arching her back so her breasts pressed into his hands. Jett ducked and kissed one breast, licking her nipple as she gasped.

"Later. We'll do things my way now."

Chapter 5

Jett stretched out on the chaise lounge, settling Anna against him. He was big and broad behind her, and she felt safe, not to mention incredibly turned on. "Mmmm, you feel good in my arms," he said, squeezing her breasts as she leaned back against his chest. She could feel his erection against her backside and squirmed, knowing she was teasing him. Jett growled behind her.

"You like teasing me," he drawled. It wasn't a question. She'd partially stripped in front of him, hadn't she? His thumbs ran over her nipples, and she moaned.

"That's right, sweetness. You're mine tonight."

"Just tonight?" she asked.

One large hand cupped the front of her neck, his thumb running over her throat as her head fell back on his shoulder. Jett liked being in control. That much was obvious. She wanted to tease him further but was having a difficult time even thinking coherently. Clearly, he knew his way around a woman's body. She felt like putty in his hands.

His thumb massaged her throat again, his other hand cupping her breast. "You can stay as long as you want, sweetheart. I can't think of anything more appealing than exploring this gorgeous body every night. Than pleasuring you. Let's take these little panties off," he murmured, one hand dropping to the black lace. "I want to see all of you."

Shifting slightly, she tugged them off without thought, letting her heels fall to the ground as well. Jett was a far better lover than most of the men she'd been with, and the night had barely even gotten started. He adjusted her against him on the plush lounge chair, hooking her legs over his own. She was spread wide open. Naked. Vulnerable. The lights in the hot tub danced as the water bubbled. Insects hummed in the night and dark woods behind them. The air felt steamy and electric. Maybe she should've been cold, but Jett was heating her body and soul. He was warming her from the inside with his compliments and commands. She wasn't the type of woman to submit to a man, but holy hell. This one knew exactly what he was doing.

Anna's head fell against his shoulder again, and she arched against him, pushing her breasts further into his grasp. Jett growled behind her. "I like you here in my arms, but now I can't taste those pretty nipples," he complained. She whimpered as he rubbed his thumbs over them. "You're sensitive," he said, his voice gruff. "I love how you respond to me."

"I love your hands on me," she admitted. She wanted to look down and see his big hands on her breasts, but she was too relaxed to move. Relaxed and completely aroused.

"I've wanted to touch you all night. You feel so good, sweetness." One hand cupped a full breast, and the other trailed down her stomach. Lower. She held her breath, waiting, and then his thick fingers were fingering her sex, trailing through her arousal. "This sweet little clit is mine, isn't it honey?" he asked, rubbing it oh-so-gently. She shuddered. She actually shuddered in his arms. "You're already wet for me. I'm going to make you come, Anna. I want to hear you shouting my name."

He held her against him, and then he was driving her crazy, rubbing small circles around her swollen bud as she gasped and heat washed over her. Jett's fingers slid through her wetness. She was slick and swollen for him, her body ready for whatever he had in store. Jett circled her clit faster, and she gasped, arching against him. Anna couldn't even control her reactions if she wanted. Her hips were lightly thrusting against his touch, her body bending to his will.

"Jett," she pleaded.

"You need my cock? You're going to come first, honey. More than once. I'm not taking you until you're begging me." Two thick fingers slid to her core, slowly pushing in. She cried out, unable to stop the sensations washing over her. His thumb slid over her clit as his fingers penetrated her. Thick. Deep. Jett shifted slightly, spreading her legs even wider. His hand squeezed her breast. "I love touching you, teasing you," he murmured. "You're too sexy for your own good. I could spend hours playing with your gorgeous body."

"God. Jett." She whimpered and gasped, flushed and hot for him but needing even more. Her body clenched down around him, and she nearly wailed at the sweet pleasure he was giving her.

"Shhh, baby. I'll take care of you."

His thumb on her clit strummed faster, his fingers fucking her harder. She was so wet, she could hear his movements. He pinched her nipple, rubbing his thumb over her clit, and then suddenly she exploded, screaming out into the dark night as Jett made her come harder than she ever had before.

Jett growled in approval, nipping at her neck. His strength and scent surrounded her, and she felt practically dizzy as she came down from that intense high. Her pussy was still spasming, and she was in shock at how well he could play her body. "Oh my God. Oh God."

"You're so tight. You're still squeezing me." He caressed her clit again and then slid his hand from her sex, sucking her juices off his thick fingers. "Mmmm. So damn sweet." She tried to adjust her legs, but he readjusted her as he stood, cradling her close to his muscular body. Anna was naked and vulnerable, but he held her close and kissed her softly.

The door shut behind them as he walked back through the house, his hot tub long forgotten. It was quiet. Intimate. They were alone in the woods, miles away from anyone else, and she'd never felt safer or more at peace.

Jett entered the large master bedroom, carrying her with ease. He tugged the dark bedspread back with one hand and lay her down in his sheets, his lips quirking as he looked down at her. "You look good in my bed."

"I'd look better with you here next to me."

"Hell, sweetness. The things I want to do to you…." He leaned closer, tugging her to the edge of the bed as he knelt down. Her legs dangled over the edge, her breath quickening.

"Jett."

He kissed her belly, slowly working his way down to her pussy lips. His fingers wrapped around her ankles, pushing her legs back, as he edged between her thighs. Her sex was exposed, bare to him, and she was at his complete mercy.

"I've been wanting to taste you," he murmured. "I want to kiss your sweet little clit every night."

"Jett," she whispered.

He leaned closer, his breath on her core.

"I'll never do anything you don't want, sweetheart. You know that, right? I'd never hurt you."

"I know," she panted, "I'm just—I need—"

"I know what you need," he said roughly. And then he was devouring her. Kissing and licking, the stubble on his jaw rubbing against her sensitized skin. She'd just come moments ago, but he already had her on the edge once again. She couldn't believe the way he kissed and nipped at her swollen folds. He was both rough and gentle at the same time, giving and taking. His tongue plundered her, penetrating her core as she cried out.

"Oh God. What are you doing to me?" she pleaded. "I can't—I just—"

He took his time, thrusting his tongue in and out. She sensed his smile more than felt it when he answered her. "I'm making you mine." Two fingers slid inside her tight channel, stretching her, and then he was sucking her clit into his mouth. Gently biting down. Anna screamed in his bedroom, Jett never letting up as he took every last ounce of pleasure.

When she was gasping for breath, he shifted her again, moving her body as if she weighted nothing. Her head rested on his pillow, his scent surrounding her. Jett stripped off his clothing, and then his muscled body prowled over her own. He was hot and hard—everywhere. Broad shoulders. A smattering of chest hair across strong pecs. The veins on his forearms and hands stood out, but my God. It was the look in his eyes that nearly slayed her. "I'm going to take you, sweet Anna," he murmured, ducking to kiss her neck. "Tell me now if you want me to stop."

Another kiss. A nip as his teeth grazed her sensitive skin.

"Sweet?" she asked, gasping as his erection brushed against her core.

"You're sweet all over," he murmured. "Soft and tempting and too good for a hardened man like me. I want you anyway though," he said roughly.

"Jett," she pleaded, her arms wrapping around his strong shoulders.

"Tell me yes," he said.

"Yes. Please."

He'd already sheathed himself, and then Jett lined himself up at her core, hot, hard, and throbbing. Thick fingers wove between hers, and he pinned her hands to the bed. Dark eyes bore into hers. And then he kissed her, slow and sweet as the head of his cock eased in.

"You're tight, honey," he said, releasing one of her hands. He adjusted one of her legs, opening her wider to him.

"God. You're big," she gasped.

"Umm-hmmm," he murmured between kisses. Gentle. Patient. "And you're hot, wet, and perfect."

She relaxed slightly, giving in to his intimate invasion as Jett penetrated her. She was full. So full. Was he bigger than other men she'd been with? Or was she so flushed and swollen with desire it only felt that way? She couldn't move, couldn't escape the pleasure he gave her. He was stretching her, and she felt like she'd die from the exquisite pressure. His thick cock moved in and out slowly, marking her. Making her his.

Jett wrapped her leg around his hip and then pinned her other hand again. She cried out with desire and his lips once again captured her own. Jett moved faster, harder. She couldn't come again. It wasn't possible. He couldn't possibly—Jett shifted and rubbed the base of his shaft against her clit. Her body began to shake from the intensity, from the unstoppable orgasm, and she screamed. Anna clung to his hands like they were her lifeline, like she'd float away if he didn't keep hold of her. He kissed her again, harder, stealing her breath. Her pussy spasmed around him. Finally, Jett stiffened slightly and came as well, nearly collapsing on top of her after his release.

He rolled to the side, taking Anna with him. She lay sprawled atop his body, panting and sweaty and dazed.

"Sweet Anna," he murmured, his hands running over her body. Jett was still half hard inside her, and she was breathless, wondering how she'd ever be able to leave this man.

Chapter 6

Anna blinked, stretching languorously the following morning. Jett's side of the bed was rumpled, and she heard the shower running in the master bathroom. It was early. Too early to be awake. How the man had made love to her for hours late last night and then gotten up so early was a mystery. She closed her eyes, smiling to herself. This was the most relaxed she'd felt in ages. There were no car horns honking outside her studio apartment. There was no noise from the neighbors' voices or thumping against the wall as the couple next door had sex. There was no music. No traffic. Just the sweet, sweet sound of silence.

She looked at the clock on his nightstand in the dim morning light. Even his bedroom was meticulously neat and clean. Organized and precise like the man himself. He must have something like one-thousand thread count sheets, because they felt much more comfortable than hers. His big king-sized bed felt amazing.

But oh God. Last night. Those hands and lips and…. She'd lost track of how many times he'd made her come. Jett was a skilled and attentive lover—a man compared to the mere boys she'd been with in the past. Sure, they might've been around her age, but they didn't stack up to him in the least.

She blinked, listening to the sound of the shower. She could go join him, but it was oh so comfy here in his bedroom. Anna closed her eyes for a moment and drifted back off to sleep.

"I made you breakfast," Jett said in a low voice, setting a tray of food on the nightstand. She heard the clink of silverware against a plate and smelled something amazing. Anna blinked sleepily, looking over at him. Jett was standing there in a clean tee shirt and pair of jeans, the stubble on his jaw making him look ruggedly handsome. His face was soft, however, as he watched her wake up.

"You did not," she said with a yawn. "I'm dreaming. You did not just give me the most amazing orgasms of my life last night and then cook breakfast for me."

He chuckled quietly. "I absolutely did—on both counts. Let me help you sit up, sweetness. You're probably sore this morning." Anna shot him a withering look, causing his sexy lips to quirk.

"I apologize if I got carried away," he said as he got her situated, his gaze dropping to where the sheet barely concealed her breasts.

She waved her hand with a little flourish. "See? I'm fine. I can sit up in bed, no problem." Jett took one of her hands gently in his own, turning it over. He ducked and kissed her wrist. Her palm. Heat began to wash over her. Without even trying, this guy was smolderingly sexy. Maybe some women would feel embarrassed to be sitting here naked, save for the sheets, but with the look Jett was giving her, she felt like she might go up in flames.

"We'll relax in the hot tub later," he said. "That'll help. I wasn't sure what you liked for breakfast, so I made a variety."

She ignored his comment about the hot tub. Jett was big. Thick. She was indeed slightly sore this morning from their lovemaking, but she certainly wasn't about to admit that to him. Nor was she going to complain about it. This man had left her a hundred percent satisfied. She didn't feel anxious or unsettled sitting here in his bedroom though. She wasn't in a rush to throw on her clothes and leave. If anything, it felt oddly comfortable. Routine even, like this scene had played out with him a thousand times.

How could Anna feel so at home with a man she'd just met?

Her eyes landed on the tray of food, her stomach reminding her she hadn't eaten since dinner. There was a plate of scrambled eggs, bacon, and toast; a bowl of fresh fruit; coffee; orange juice; yogurt; and a croissant. "Where's your food?" she asked. "This can't all be for me."

"I already ate. Early riser," he said with a wink.

She took the mug of coffee, smiling at him. "And what did you do all morning while I relaxed in your bed? Aside from cooking for me, that is."

Jett sank down onto the bed, running his hand over her leg. Even through the sheet, she could feel the heat of his touch. "I had some work to do, assignments to give my men. I might have a meeting tomorrow."

"On a Sunday?"

"We'll see. Duty calls. Hazard of running your own business. I had one of my assistants drop off some clothes for you."

"You didn't!"

His lips quirked again. "I did. It's too cold to swim in the lake, but I thought you might want to see the property. It's gorgeous in the fall with the leaves changing color. As appealing as I found those sexy heels, I doubt you'd want to walk around in the grass in them. My shoes are obviously too big to fit you."

"Very much so," Anna agreed. "You know what they say, big shoes, big…." She trailed off, smiling at him playfully.

"You're trouble," he said with a chuckle. "And don't forget to text your friends this morning to let them know you're okay."

"Are you always this bossy?"

"Always," he agreed.

She burst into laughter, unable to help herself. Every time she tried to one-up this man, he had a quick comeback. She snagged a piece of bacon, taking a bite. "God, this is good. Not too dry and crisp, but absolutely perfect. Ohhh, be careful, Jett. I could get used to a man cooking me breakfast."

He smiled back at her, a twinkle in his eyes. "I could get used to cooking for you, especially if you're here in my bed." A flicker of something passed between them. He clearly couldn't cook for her every day. She lived in the city. But she absolutely didn't mind him spoiling her like this.

They talked as she ate some of her breakfast, Anna only tugging the sheets back into place once. It felt indulgent to be relaxing naked between the sheets while Jett was fully dressed. He wasn't complaining though. Anna didn't miss the ways his eyes heated when he looked at her, briefly gazing at her cleavage. He was being a gentleman at the moment, but he was still a red-blooded male.

"I want to ask you something, but I understand if you don't want to answer."

Jett raised his eyebrows. "What? Is there something you need?"

"How many women do you bring here? Seriously. Like, is this an every week type of thing? Or maybe every time you're in the city?"

"I've never brought a woman here," he said, those dark eyes pinning her in place.

"You're joking."

"I'm not saying I never date or spend the night with a woman, but here? No. You're the first, Anna. What can I say? When I saw you at the bar last night, there was just something I couldn't resist. You can't tell me you click with every man you meet the way we did."

"No, not at all. I just figured you're so smooth you must do this all the time."

His hand briefly rubbed her leg through the sheet. It wasn't sexual. If anything, it was almost meant to be comforting. Reassuring. "Never. I wouldn't lie about that. You're the first woman I've ever brought to my house."

A warmth filled her chest as she watched him. She didn't get the vibe that he was lying. Why lie about this? She was already here. They'd already slept together. "Hmmm," she said noncommittally. She wasn't entirely sure what to make of his admission.

"I'll bring in the clothes my assistant dropped off. I didn't want to wake you earlier."

"So what are we going to see outside? The lake?" she asked hopefully.

Jett nodded. "If you'd like. We arrived last night when it was dark, so I'm sure you'd like to see where exactly we are."

"Absolutely. I'm sure it's amazing. You know what I don't miss here? The cars honking. The traffic. My neighbors talking and thumping against the wall while they have sex." Jett looked surprised for a beat but burst into laughter. "Why would you ever meet your clients in the city?" she continued. "You should bring them all up here."

He watched her with amusement. "My office is nearby, too. Sometimes I have meetings with my clients there."

"Shadow Security? No. Aren't we in the middle of nowhere?"

"Upstate is hardly the middle of nowhere, sweetness." He reached over and snagged a strawberry slice from the bowl, holding it up to her.

"So now you're going to feed me breakfast?"

"You're talking more than eating," he said, moving his fingers toward her lips. She let him feed her the strawberry, staring at him as she swallowed, and Jett ran his thumb over her lips. It was intimate. Bold. Jett made her feel like she was his.

Anna's heartbeat increased as he ducked in for a kiss, the sheets falling away from her breasts with his movement. "Ah, much better," he joked, lightly palming one breast as he kissed her again. "You're far too tempting."

Anna playfully swatted at his hand. "You might

have been joking about my being sore, but I actually am."

"I'm sorry," he said, looking slightly chastised. "I'll be good—for now."

Anna let the sheets lay in her lap, continuing to eat the fruit as if she wasn't sitting there in his bed naked.

"Woman," he growled.

"What?" she asked innocently, popping another piece of fruit in her mouth. "Is this a problem?

He shook his head, muttering a curse, but she could see the smile he was trying to hide. It was going to be fun teasing Jett today. She had a feeling he wasn't used to it. Jett was the type of man who liked to be in control—to call all the shots. His employees probably did what he wanted, no questions asked. He didn't seem to mind when she challenged him. Anna was looking forward to spending the day with Jett, getting to know the man better. He made her laugh, but that didn't explain the crazy draw she felt toward him or the continuous hum of electricity arcing between them. Things would never be boring with him and something about that captivated her.

**

"You're ready," Jett said, looking up from his kitchen table as Anna strode in. He left his laptop open, watching her spin in a circle. His assistant Lena had done well selecting clothes for her. He owed her big time for managing to round up some clothing this early on a Saturday morning. Fortunately, he had connections. The shop owner was happy to open the store for a small fee. The jeans Anna had on hugged her sexy ass, and the cashmere sweater and boots she wore would be fine for outside. She smiled at him, and Jett knew she enjoyed the way he watched her.

"What are you working on?"

"I had to brief my team on something. Now I'm just finishing up a document I'm sending a client. Nothing classified."

"Oh, and your security company usually deals with that?"

He smiled, not answering. Better to let her assume what she wanted than explain the details of his operations. "I've about had it with this file though. Usually someone else works on these damn things, but I had a last-minute item to send."

"Just highlight the section and clear the formatting," she said, looking over his shoulder at the mess on the screen.

Jett raised his eyebrows but tried it, muttering in surprise when it worked. "Well thank God. Now I can send this actually looking semi-polished, and we can get on with our day." He shut his laptop and looked up at her. "Tell me you texted your friends."

"That I did," she said with a big grin. "But don't worry, I didn't kiss and tell about exactly how amazing the night was."

"No?" he asked, feeling amused.

She took his hand and tugged him up from his chair, surprising him. "No, I'd rather keep you to myself," Anna said. Jett shook his head, smiling, but ducked down and kissed her. He needed to be careful. As different as they were, he could see himself falling for a woman like Anna. Jett didn't have time for a serious relationship, but hell. Having Anna here was as close as he'd gotten recently to wanting one. He was attracted to her, but she kept him on his toes.

Made him feel alive. Yes, he had work, but there was more to life than that, wasn't there?

"So, are you going to show me around?" she asked, breathing heavily as they came up for air. He reluctantly released her.

"That I will. Let me set the alarm before we go out."

"I guess that's the hazard of running your own security business—you're always overly concerned about security."

"Overly concerned?"

She shrugged. "This is almost the middle of nowhere. I lock my door in Manhattan, but I live in a building full of strangers. Anyone could try to break in."

Jett frowned. She was right. Of course, she lived amongst strangers. He had, too, back in his military days. That was how apartment life worked. A beautiful woman alone in the city was different than his being alone. He was a large man. He didn't like the thought of someone trying to enter her studio apartment. "Do you know your neighbors?"

"Some. I'm not at home that much to see them. I've been putting in twelve-hour days lately, which blows."

"Has your boss been hounding you today?"

"He did text me this morning. I forwarded him yet another report I already sent this week. What can I do? If I send what he needs, I won't get a zillion texts or calls demanding I get it to him. I think he's just too lazy to sift through his emails."

He mulled over that as he pocketed his cell phone and keys. Anna had seemed stressed when he'd first met her yesterday, but who wasn't tired after the long workweek by Friday night? He loved seeing how relaxed and carefree she was here. Hell, after a few drinks together, she'd seemed happier. Lighter. He treated his own employees well, but that was neither here nor there. It's not like she'd be working for him.

"Let's go check out the lake and then enjoy lunch," Jett said. "I'll have one of my staff drop something off."

"No more cooking for me?" she joked.

Jett's eyes heated as he looked at her. "If you behave, I'll make dinner for us tonight."

She giggled. "And if not?"

Jett snagged her hand, guiding her toward the back door. "Don't tempt me, woman," he mock-growled. His hand landed on her ass as he guided her outside, but Anna just laughed harder. She probably would enjoy tempting him, seeing what she could get away with. This woman.

"It's beautiful," she said as they stepped onto the stone patio and looked around. "I didn't get a good look last night since we were, uh, preoccupied."

"Are you complaining?" he asked, a smile playing about his lips as he glanced over to the chaise lounge. He'd gathered her clothes earlier but realized her panties were still on the ground.

She smirked. "Keeping those as a souvenir? Too bad. They're my favorite pair, so I'm taking them with me when I go." Jett stiffened slightly but followed her across the patio area as she continued taking in the surroundings. Of course, she was going to go. She couldn't stay here forever. She worked in the city. That didn't stop the slight twinge of regret at her mentioning it. He couldn't remember the last time he'd so thoroughly enjoyed an evening with a woman—and it wasn't just because of the sex, although that had been incredible.

Jett liked having Anna here. He didn't want to examine that thought too closely.

"So, why'd you move way up here?" she asked as they headed across his lawn toward the lake and beyond.

Jett took her hand, enjoying having Anna close. "I like my privacy. I didn't want my company headquarters to be in the city or any of the boroughs. I like having some land and peace. I've got kayaks and a boat to enjoy here. I can relax by the firepit or enjoy my hot tub. I set up my headquarters nearby. I can get into the city if I need to. I do miss skiing though. I actually just bought a cabin out west."

"Wait, you have this gorgeous home surrounded by woods, and you bought a cabin?"

"It's in ski country. I'll rent it out. It's an investment, but I can fly out there whenever I want during ski season and hit the slopes."

"God. I'm terrible at skiing."

He smiled down at her. "I doubt that."

"Well, maybe not terrible. I probably just don't ski enough to actually be good at it. Besides, my parents are in Florida now. Some vacations I'll visit them and then go spend some time at a nice beach resort, soaking up the sun."

"There's plenty of those in Florida."

"Exactly. I haven't taken a vacation all year though—just quick weekends here and there." She let out a sigh, glancing across the water as they walked. They'd left the dock and patio area behind but were still on his land. He hadn't mentioned the fences he had surrounding his entire property. The security this private home afforded him.

"Why haven't you taken a vacation?" he asked.

"My boss is a dick. He wouldn't grant me a week's vacation this summer, saying he needed me at the office. He's in the middle of a divorce and has a mistress or two. I keep things running for him."

They'd walked ten minutes from the house while they were talking, Anna's hand still in his, Jett realized in surprise. Although he wasn't the type of man that typically held hands with a woman, he was surprised that he enjoyed the connection between them. She was young and refreshing compared to his jaded views of the world.

"Does the wife know about the mistresses?"

"Oh, she knows. I've gotten an earful before because she thought I was sleeping with him, too."

"You don't sound like you love your job very much," Jett said.

"It's a job. Who loves work? It pays the bills."

His thumb swiped over her skin. He could understand that. While he'd appreciated the value in serving his country, listening to the military chain of command wasn't his thing either. Now he completed missions on his own terms. Running his own black ops team let him remain in control. He picked the operations. He called the shots. "I can't complain about running Shadow Security," he admitted. "I picked my employees and take jobs that I want."

"That's different," she said.

"Yes and no." He didn't bother explaining. He might not always love the complications of having a cover for his black ops team, but he made it work. Not every employee knew what went on behind closed doors. They assumed the men were providing security for certain situations or people. But taking out dangerous men? Conducting missions the government wouldn't? He was sure that hadn't crossed their minds. His Shadow Ops Team was the best of the best. Most people would never know what they did, and he was fine with it.

His mind ran over the email he'd sent earlier. He needed to meet with another government official in a few days. There were new problems arising, new missions to take on. That didn't even include his meetings in New York yesterday.

They kept walking for another fifteen minutes in companionable silence. It was peaceful. A far cry from life in the city. Finally, his destination came into view. Anna smiled as she realized a picnic blanket was spread out on the ground ahead of them. Jett had asked Lena to purchase some food, pillows, and blankets so they could relax outside and enjoy lunch together. The fact that it was secluded and romantic was an added bonus.

"Jett!" Anna said excitedly. "You did not make a picnic for us."

"I didn't," he admitted. "But I had my assistant set everything up."

Anna playfully elbowed him, and Jett couldn't resist pulling her close. "I told you I wasn't making lunch for us." He kept his arm wrapped around her as they walked the rest of the way toward the set up. Lena had outdone herself. There was an actual goddamn picnic basket, champagne chilling in a bucket, plush pillows, blankets, and even some candles. Jett realized he'd never once picnicked on his property before. Why would he? If the team came over, they'd spend time in the house or on the large patio. He'd order food or have something prepared. Most likely, they'd be at headquarters, mulling over their latest op. If he was with a woman, he'd fly her off somewhere exotic.

They slowed as they came to the blanket. Unable to resist, Jett let his hand slide to Anna's ass, where he gave her a gentle squeeze. He swore he couldn't keep his hands off this woman. She had tempting curves on that willowy frame. She turned toward him and smiled, slow and sultry. "Like what you see?" she teased.

"You know I do," he said huskily. "Lunch first though. Have a seat," he said, helping her to the ground. Jett sank down beside her, his chest swelling at the happy look on her face. He doubted any of the men she'd dated set up an elaborate picnic like this. Most guys wouldn't go through the trouble. He popped the cork on the champagne, pouring her a glass.

"Mmm, this is good," she said, her eyes shining with excitement as she took a sip.

Jett opened the picnic basket, pulling out an assortment of food. There were sandwiches, cheese, crackers, and more fruit. Chocolates for dessert. "Your assistant set this up?" Anna asked.

"She did," Jett said, handing Anna a plate.

"Well, give the woman a raise," Anna replied with an easy laugh. Jett watched her help herself to some food. He struck a match and lit some of the candles. He had to hand it to Lena—they were a nice touch. They were in some type of glass vase so they wouldn't blow out or tip over, and he looked over the setup approvingly.

"Hurricane lanterns," Anna explained when she

caught him looking at them. "Who knew you were into such rustic chic?"

"Not me," Jett muttered.

Anna picked up a slice of brie, taking a bite. She looked so damn beautiful sitting amongst the pillows—relaxed. Happy. Although she'd been attractive yesterday, sleek and polished, he loved her in casual clothes, too, with minimal makeup. He assumed she'd had that in her purse, since he hadn't purchased anything like that. Her cheeks were flushed, her eyes bright. She was naturally beautiful though. His chest tightened.

"Good?" he asked, watching as she daintily took another bite of brie.

"The best."

Jett helped himself to some food, starting with a sandwich. He wasn't much for frou-frou stuff like brie, but he had to admit, he appreciated that Anna was clearly enjoying herself. His mind wandered back to feeding her strawberries in bed this morning. As much as he'd wanted to make love to her then, he'd known she was sore. She probably still was. That didn't mean he wouldn't love to feast on her after they'd eaten.

They talked for a while during lunch, savoring their meal. Jett snagged a chocolate when she'd finished what was on her plate, holding it up to her mouth. She flashed him a look but then willingly let him feed her. It was intimate. Private. She took a sip of her champagne, watching him. Jett fed her another small chocolate, letting his thumb trail over her lips. Her cheeks were flushed, her chest rising and falling. And she still smelled like those damn peaches. So fucking sweet. He moved in for a kiss, tasting the alcohol and dessert, mixed in with the sweetness that was pure Anna. Jett eased her back onto the pillows, loving how her body relaxed beneath his. He'd underestimated how much he'd enjoy stretching her out on a blanket in his massive yard. She was like a present waiting to be unwrapped.

He kissed her leisurely, in no hurry, loving the feel of her body beneath his.

"Mmmm, you're ready to go," she teased, feeling his erection brush against her.

Jett nipped at her neck. "Yes, but I can be good. This is about you." He kissed her neck again, moving his lips higher. Anna gasped as he nibbled just below her ear. Anna was sensitive everywhere. Her nipples. The backs of her knees. Her pussy. He'd explored her thoroughly last night, enjoying how she gave herself over to him. He could get lost in a woman like her. It was dangerous yet exhilarating. He'd focused on his career his entire damn life. Traveled around the world. Who knew he could feel so content relaxing on his own property with a woman?

"Jett," she pleaded as his teeth grazed her neck. Her hips shifted slightly.

He moved down her body obligingly. Jett lifted her sweater a few inches, kissing her belly. It was cool outside, and he grabbed one of the blankets to keep her warm. His fingers deftly undid the button on her jeans before he slid the zipper down. "I need to taste you," he murmured. Jett tugged the denim and her panties down to her calves, pausing to remove her boots. He tugged her jeans the rest of the way off her smooth legs, enjoying the feel of her soft skin beneath his fingertips. Jett draped her legs over his shoulders, loving the way she gasped as he moved closer.

"Let's see how quickly I can make you come," he said huskily, before feasting on the delectable woman in front of him. Anna tried to conceal her cries, but Jett licked and laved at her until she was writhing in pleasure. She was wet and pink and perfect. So damn sweet it killed him. He kissed her pussy like she was his—as if she were made for him alone.

Anna was clutching onto the blankets, crying out. Jett sucked her swollen clit into his mouth, loving the way she arched up against him. His tongue flicked against her tender nub.

"Oh God. Jett. Jett!"

Male pride surged through him as she screamed out her release. He continued to gently lap at her pussy, bringing her down from that orgasmic high. Anna was panting and breathless, her blonde hair spread around her head like an angel, her sex inches from his lips. She was soft and sweet. Willing. So damn right. It would be hell having to let her go.

Chapter 7

Anna relaxed in Jett's hot tub late that night, texting her friends while he sent off another email. He'd promised to rejoin her shortly, but after an amazing dinner together on his patio, she was content to relax while he worked a bit. They hadn't even discussed heading back to the city tonight. It was hard to imagine returning to the real world tomorrow. She'd known him barely more than twenty-four hours, and it was like nothing in her life was the same.

He looked up from where he sat at the patio table, smiling. "What?" she asked innocently.

"You. In my hot tub. I like it."

She leaned over and set her phone on the table, giving him an eyeful of her bare breasts. Jett muttered under his breath, and she smiled. "Almost finished?"

"Yeah. In more ways than one."

Anna burst into laughter as he adjusted himself in his boxers. While they'd both been in the hot tub naked earlier, he'd pulled boxers on to send a few emails. He finished typing and then flipped his laptop shut. "There. All done." His eyes landed on their glasses of wine as he stood up. Then he was stripping bare in front of her, climbing in with a smile.

"Do you always work so hard?" she asked as he sank down onto the bench beside her. The water bubbled around them, and his arm easily slipped around her shoulders. She leaned into him, content. It was peaceful out here, with the dim lights around the patio and night sky overhead. It had cooled down a bit since yesterday, but Jett and the hot tub were keeping her warm.

Jett mindlessly played with her hair as she rested against him. It felt like they'd done this a million times before—like it was normal to spend Saturday evening naked together on his patio. It was surprising to spend so much time with another person yet have no desire to leave. Normally Anna craved her space. Jett made her feel...like herself. Content and safe. It made no sense. She enjoyed going out with her friends but had always been happy on her own. Jett felt like her other half. Something about them just fit together in a way words couldn't describe.

"Usually, I'm working more," he admitted. "Today is the most time I've afforded myself to relax in months. How about you?"

She shrugged, Jett's eyes landing on her cleavage with the movement. "That was my boss texting me earlier."

"What? I thought you were texting your friends."

"I was, but then he needed some file and didn't think a thing of bothering me about it on a Saturday night."

"So you sent it?"

"No, I don't have a copy. I'd have to go into the office, which I'm definitely not doing." Anna jumped as her phone began to buzz on the table. "Speaking of the guy, that's him."

She swiped the screen. "Anna Dubois." She watched Jett's lips quirk from the corner of her eye. He didn't move from where he sat with his arm around her shoulder, just let her take the call, naked beside him. Her lips twitched. Her boss was rambling on and on, but she was finding it hard to even care. Anna had been fed up for months with her ever-increasing workload and his demands. It was one thing to deal with his ineptitude during the work day, but now? This was at least the fourth weekend in a row he'd wanted her to go into the office.

"No, I can't get that document to you tonight. It's filed in the office, and I don't have an electronic version given the sensitivity of it."

"I need you to head over there right now. The security guys will let you in. I don't have a copy at my penthouse, and it's urgent."

Anna rolled her eyes. Her boss and his family lived in an expensive townhouse. If he was at his penthouse, it was because he was with his mistress for the weekend. "Unfortunately, I'm unavailable as I'm not in the city this evening."

She held her phone away from her ear as he began cursing.

"It's not possible for me to return tonight. Perhaps someone else will be available to send it to you."

"You're my fucking executive assistant," he said, starting another tirade. "I pay you to work for me, not the other way around. Get the damn document to me tonight!"

Jett stiffened beside her, no doubt hearing the exchange. Anna was gripping her cell phone so tightly, her hand was turning white. She'd had enough. Enough of all of it. Enough of the texts and phone calls and emails. Enough of sending him the same damn thing multiple times. If he wanted to screw half of Manhattan, this was his problem. He was too busy thinking with his dick to keep his work affairs in order. The document was probably at his home, with his wife.

"If that's the way you feel, then I quit. Effective immediately."

"Anna, wait, I need you—"

"I'll turn in my credentials on Monday. Goodbye."

She ended the call and then shut off her phone, bristling. Jett was watching her quietly but was smart enough not to comment. Anna huffed out a breath, tossing her phone onto the table and leaning back into the hot tub. "He's an asshole," she said. "That probably seemed impulsive and rash, but I've been thinking about quitting for months. That just sealed the deal. Last weekend the security guys let me in at three in the morning to get something to him. Life is too short to keep that up. He's like an overgrown man-child who needs all the women around him to get his shit together."

Jett chuckled softly, pulling her against him. She let him hold her in his arms and realized she was practically vibrating with anger and adrenaline. "You must think I'm crazy," she said, letting out a sigh.

His large hand smoothed down over the back of her head. "I think nothing of the sort. You were fed up with that prick when I met you. If he's always such an ass, then you can do better. It's a big world. No need to keep a job you loathe."

"Yeah, well, I'd planned to find a new job before quitting that one, but c'est la vie." She huffed out a breath against his skin, suddenly realizing that she was naked in his lap. Jett continued smoothing her hair, the water swirling around them, but she felt his cock twitch beneath her ass. Heat and awareness washed over her. She twisted so that she was straddling him, watching his lips curl up in amusement. Jett's arms locked around her, and his cock swelled beneath her pussy. She shamelessly rubbed herself against him, loving that Jett leaned down to kiss her.

She wrapped her arms around his shoulders, pulling him close.

"I didn't bring a condom outside, sweetness. I'm clean, but are you on the pill?"

"IUD," she said between heated kisses. "I'm clean, too."

He kissed her more deeply then, his hands firmly gripping her hips. Anna wiggled against him, feeling her slickened folds brush against his erection. Jett lifted her up slightly in the water, and then he was pulling her down. Plunging into her body. She gasped at his penetration and then relaxed around him, taking his impressive girth until he was fully seated inside her. "Are you sore?" he murmured.

"I'll survive."

"I'll be gentle." Jett's hands slid to her ass as she clung to his shoulders, and then she was riding him, their lovemaking slow and sweet in the swirling water. He kissed her gently. Softly. His thick cock filled her, touching every nerve ending inside, but as promised, it was slow. Sweet. Her entire body was alight with awareness, every movement sending shockwaves right through her. Jett didn't let up, just slowly eased in and out of her core. His thumb gently strummed her clit. Soft. Patient. When she came, she clung to him as Jett murmured into her ear. She was gasping and wrapped around Jett like she was his. He held her body close as he came as well and then stood with her in his arms, his cock sliding free from her body.

The night air kissed her wet skin, pebbling her nipples. Jett wrapped her in a warm blanket as she shivered and then carried her inside, tucking her into his bed. "I guess I'm staying tonight," she murmured sleepily.

Jett climbed in beside her, pulling her close. His arms wrapped around her from behind, one hand cupping her breast. "Stay as long as you want, sweetness." He kissed her bare shoulder, leaving her smiling as she fell asleep safe in his arms.

Chapter 8

"What do you mean you quit?" Ashleigh asked in surprise the next day.

"Exactly that. I quit," Anna said with a rueful laugh, adjusting her phone as she stretched out on Jett's sofa. "My boss called last night and wanted me to get something from the office for him at ten p.m. It was ridiculous. Last week Mike the security guy let me in in the middle of the night to send him some papers. I've also been there several other weekends this month. I'm done. Twelve-hour days are enough. I'm not paid enough to be there late at night and on weekends, too."

"Wow. I mean, good for you. I've been saying you can do better. I know the pay was decent, but yikes. The hours were awful for you."

"That they were," Anna agreed. "He was shocked, but I've had enough. I'll turn in my access card tomorrow and clear out my stuff."

She brushed back a piece of hair as she relaxed, watching Jett move around the kitchen. He was cooking a late brunch for them, much to her surprise. He'd actually stayed in bed with her this morning, holding her close. They'd talked quietly and simply been content to be together. They hadn't made love since last night, which was fine. It almost frightened her how tender he'd been in the hot tub. That was crazy. It was hot tub sex. Vacation sex—well, a weekend fling at any rate. Jett making love to her gently shouldn't make her feel things that didn't exist. Still, they'd spent nearly every moment together since Friday evening, and she felt a tiny tugging in her chest at having to get back to reality, to going back to her own cramped space.

"So, you are back home from your night away?" Ashleigh teased. "I figured you'd call me sometime yesterday."

"Not exactly," Anna said with a slow smile. "I'm still at Jett's."

"What?!" Ashleigh practically shrieked. "You've been at his place since Friday night?"

Her lips quirked. "Yep. It's been...amazing, actually. It was impulsive to go home with him, but it's flown by. We just click, as cliché as that is. He's cooked for me, shown me around his property. We talk and laugh. And the sex is spectacular," she added in a whisper.

Ashleigh giggled. "Oh my God. Well, that's one thing I'm having none of."

"Uh-huh. No complaints here."

"Well, damn. So what? He's driving you back tonight?"

"He has to. I've got to clean out my desk and job

hunt, apparently. I'm sure my boss will try to talk me into staying, but I've had it. New York is a big place. I'll find something else."

Jett came walking into the living room just then, looking sexier than any man had a right to. He wore a tee shirt and jeans, yet was barefoot. Just seeing his muscled arms and bare skin sent a skittering of awareness over her. "Want to say hi to my best friend, Ashleigh?" she asked.

Jett obligingly took the phone but put it on speaker. "Hi Ashleigh. I can assure you Anna is fine here. Does she have a curfew tonight?" he joked.

"Very funny. There's nothing wrong with worrying about my friend," Ashleigh said.

"That there's not."

"I told her I quit my job," Anna said with a smile.

"I had nothing to do with that, in case you're worried," Jett said.

"Oh, I know. Anna's impulsive and crazy, but her boss sucked. Anyway, it sounds like you're busy, Anna. I'll talk to you tonight—or whenever. Have fun, kids!"

Anna flashed him a look as she took the phone back. "She's worried about me."

"I don't blame her. You ran off with a man for the weekend." His lips quirked in amusement. "Can't say I'm complaining though. The food's ready." Jett's phone buzzed at that moment, and he pulled it from his pocket with a frown. Anna watched as he quickly thumbed a response. "Just work stuff." He held out his hand, helping her to stand up.

Anna smiled up at him. Barefoot, she only reached his chin. The heels she'd worn Friday night had been long forgotten. She felt a twinge of guilt he'd gotten her so many clothes, but the things had been perfect for the weekend. When she'd offered to pay for them, he'd immediately brushed her off. If she ever met his assistant, Anna would have to thank her. The woman did have good taste in clothes.

"It smells good," she said.

"Not as good as you," he argued, gently nuzzling her hair.

Anna smirked, pulling back. "There's time for that later. Let's eat. Someone's been keeping me busy this weekend, and I'm starving."

***

Jett walked out of the master bathroom that afternoon, frowning as his phone buzzed on his nightstand. After a leisurely brunch and hour spent talking, he'd taken Anna to bed. They'd made love slowly, passionately, and he'd hated thinking he needed to take her back to the city tonight. The idea of leaving her in that studio apartment she seemed to loathe was appalling.

He let out a sigh.

She looked like she'd fallen asleep, and the rightness of her there in his bed shocked him. He'd never needed a woman before, yet it hadn't felt stifling with her here this weekend. Yes, the sex had been amazing, but he liked talking to her, too. Jett loved the way she made him laugh and smile. She wasn't intimidated by him, which was refreshing. He'd avoided almost all thoughts of work the past twenty-four hours, but the realities of his job were that he was always busy. On alert. Ready to send his men into action.

Jett stiffened, re-reading the message on his cell phone. "Anna," he said, gently nudging her. "Something's come up, sweetness. I'll be back in an hour."

"What?" she asked, her voice soft. Anna looked drowsy and sated in his bed, like she'd been thoroughly fucked. He wasn't finished with her yet either, but this matter couldn't be ignored.

He moved closer, planting a kiss on her forehead. The covers shifted, revealing the top of one perfect, creamy breast. "I told you a little about what I do. It's urgent. Shadow Security Headquarters is near my house. Most people would assume it's a warehouse in the middle of the woods, except for the state-of-the art security surrounding it." He swiped a screen on his phone, pulling up a live feed showing the front of the building. She looked baffled as he flashed the footage at her. "I apologize. I don't usually leave a beautiful woman alone in my bed."

"Stranded here," she pointed out.

"Thoroughly sated. Relax. I need to update my team, and then I'll be back. We'll have dinner together. If you need to get back tonight, I'll drive you home afterwards."

She raised an eyebrow. "If?"

"I was serious when I said you can stay as long as you want."

"I don't have a car, Jett. I use public transportation in the city. And there's that little thing about needing to look for a new job."

"Telecommute," he said with a wink. "And hell, if a vehicle is all that's keeping you from staying longer, you can borrow one of mine."

Anna smiled, surprising him yet again. "All right.

Sounds good."

He raised an eyebrow. "I had considered you might be upset at my leaving you here in bed."

"I had an ex who'd take calls in the middle of sex—literally. We'd be in bed together, and he'd reach over and grab the phone on the nightstand if it rang. This is nothing."

Jett growled softly, bending over to kiss her pink lips. "I promise that when I'm balls deep inside you, you're the only thing on my mind, sweetness."

Her hand ran over the stubble on his jaw. "Then we're good. If you have to work while I relax on a Sunday afternoon, I'm fine with that. I was almost asleep anyway since someone's kept me up late the past few nights." She winked.

He smirked, letting his gaze rake over her. "Nights I've very much enjoyed. I'll be back soon, baby."

He turned and was walking out of his bedroom before he thought better of it. There was no reason not to leave Anna alone here. All of his work materials were at Shadow Security Headquarters or in his safe. He'd have his cell phone and laptop on his person. Not that he thought she would snoop around his home. Jett was normally a private man, but the idea of Anna here in his home, sleeping in his bed, set off a possessiveness that surprised him. He didn't want her to leave, he realized. Not at all.

They'd have to talk later on tonight.

Chapter 9

"What's up, boss?" Ford Anderson asked, looking up as Jett strode in. The large, muscular man was seated at the conference table, watching everyone else come in. The team had assembled quickly, gathering around the sleek conference room at Shadow Security. A massive screen took up the front of the space for secure video conferences and briefings. The long table was wired for the team to plug in their laptops or other electronics. A laptop sat at the front of the room for Jett to access what he needed. Other equipment was nearby as well—headphones, mics, other communications devices.

Each man on the Shadow Ops Team had an office here, and the front office staff worked during the week. Jett had employees who answered phones, made travel arrangements, and otherwise kept the office running. They weren't privy to the real work that went on though. The men did provide security sometimes, although that was usually for government officials who'd become targets. Random rich and famous people needing bodyguards weren't on his radar.

Luke Willard sank into a seat beside him, frowning. He scrubbed a hand over the dark stubble on his jaw, his blue eyes landing on the other man. "Nothing good. It's a damn Sunday afternoon."

The other men grabbed their chairs, waiting for Jett to start the briefing. The team had known the operation they were discussing today was a possibility ever since Jett's meeting in Manhattan Friday evening. Jett had gotten the papers identifying the target from his contact. They were just waiting on word from the Government to swoop in.

"It's complicated. Amir Masih is a diplomat in the U.S. who arrived nearly one year ago. He's been in Washington, D.C., traveling frequently around the country. He's also been on the government's radar for the past several months and has recently been added to the terror watchlist."

"Fuck," Sam Jackson swore, clenching his fist. He and Ford were the two biggest guys on the Shadow Ops Team—tall and muscled, the type of men no one wanted to mess with.

Jett's gaze met his. "He's been watched for the past month by Federal Agents. Tailed without his knowledge. The government has read his mail and intercepted all his electronic communications. They're ready to move in and question him. Our team is going to locate and exfil Amir. We'll fly him to a location offshore so he's no longer on U.S. soil."

"Goddamn," Nick Dowd muttered. Around six feet tall with lean muscle, his dark hair longer than in their Army days, Nick was absolutely lethal. He was the best shot of all of them, with amazing accuracy. He'd gotten them out of plenty of bad situations from the sniper's roost. Jett was damn glad he'd come to work for the Shadow Ops Team years ago. "And the Feds will interrogate him?" Nick asked.

"Someone will," Jett confirmed. "He's under diplomatic immunity as long as he's on U.S. soil. The CIA and FBI both want information from him. They could have him arrested, but they'd have to contact the embassy because he's here on a diplomatic visa. He'd be flown back to Iran before the day was up. We'd get no answers."

"What's he planning?" Luke asked.

"Simultaneous attacks on several large universities. He's been trying to recruit students to his underground terror cell. Although we'd had eyes on him, a young university student reported the incident to the FBI."

"Damn. That was smart," Sam said appreciatively.

"It was. It also sped things up for us as far as a timeline for exfiltration is concerned. We'll need a team on the ground in Seattle tomorrow. He's attending a conference there this week. Final clearance is expected to go through this evening, but we need to move now to be ready. I'll need two of you to fly to the West Coast."

Luke crossed his arms, eyeing Jett. "Do we have a plane?" He wasn't asking how they'd get to Seattle. The complication would be getting Amir out of the country.

"Working on it. We'll get a pilot to fly us out."

"Are you coming, too, boss?" Luke asked.

"Not for the exfil, but I might be in Seattle later

this week. One of my government contacts will be there, and he wants to meet in person to discuss another operation. I've actually been meaning to head out to the West Coast soon myself. I bought a cabin out there."

Ford chuckled. "Nice. Is that where we're staying?"

Jett shot him a look. "Negative. You'll be in the city. Amir's been known to enjoy a late night out at the clubs after the conference sessions are over for the day. It shouldn't be too difficult to get him alone and bring him to the airstrip."

"Fuck me," Luke muttered.

"No thanks," Jett said, causing the men around them to roar in laughter. "And I've got other news as well. I sent a contract to Gray Pierce yesterday afternoon. He's coming onboard with Shadow Security."

"About damn time," Sam said with a chuckle. "I thought that boy would never give it up."

Jett smirked, eyeing his team. "He's restless. You know as well as I do that men like us need a mission—a purpose. He was a damn good soldier. We can use his skillset."

Ford crossed his arms, leaning back in his seat. "Are we ever bringing in some of the front office staff on what we do here? It'd be nice to have someone around on the weekends to assist. The nine-to-five security gig isn't exactly how we roll."

"Agreed," Jett said, a thought crossing his mind. It had weighed on him a while that they needed more admin support. His receptionist strictly worked nine to five. Having additional support staff in place here would take some weight off his shoulders. Anna was quick-thinking and had been dedicated to her work. She'd gone into her Manhattan office at three in the morning just to send her boss some damn paperwork. He shook his head. He didn't typically mix business with pleasure, but offering her a job wouldn't be the worst thing in the world. Selfishly, he loved the idea of having her close. Having Anna in his bed wasn't exactly a hardship. But working with her? Jett always had good instincts about people. It seemed crazy to offer a job to a woman he knew next-to-nothing about. Especially a woman he wanted as badly as her.

The idea took root anyway, the possibilities stretching out before him.

"I might have someone in mind," he said. "We'll see. Clara is too sweet to get mixed up in this," he said, referring to their receptionist. "Plus, she needs normal hours." The single mother was dedicated to her work but too damn innocent to understand the depth of their work here. Jett was sure she had no clue what went on behind closed doors and would no doubt be shocked to the core. Running ops the government didn't want to get their hands dirty with took a special breed of men. Although they might be on the wrong side of the law at times, they were getting the mission done. Serving their country. Saving lives. Taking a violent terrorist off the street wouldn't cause him to lose any sleep at night.

Clara did an excellent job of answering the phones and keeping the office stocked with supplies. She booked their travel and understood they provided security. Some people did indeed call requesting security services. All the government black ops work, however, came straight through him.

Jett crossed the room, holding a stack of materials

he'd printed off. It wouldn't be bad having someone to help him with the paperwork, he realized. Someone he trusted. He tossed the packets onto the table, watching as Ford slid them to the others. "This is our guy," Jett said.

"He looks sleazy," Sam commented.

"He's fucking at least three of the conference attendees."

"What the hell kind of conference is this?" Ford asked in amusement.

Luke elbowed him. "Looking to get some action?"

Jett's gaze slid to them. "Academia. That's how he's getting information on the universities. Although he's here on a diplomatic visa, he was taking some graduate courses as well. No doubt it was all a cover for the terror cell he's now trying to form."

Jett pulled up some information on his laptop, showing it to the men on the large screen. He went through the timeline of how the takedown would occur. "Who wants point on this operation?" he asked.

"I'm in," Ford said, his gaze narrowing. "That jackass just looks like a sleazy mofo. The sooner we get him to the Feds, the better."

"Me too," Sam agreed. "I'm in."

"All right. I'll arrange cover and have Clara book flights. You'll fly commercial to Seattle. You'll be leaving the country by other means, of course. I'll get a pilot on standby. The Feds will meet you at the black site. They're working out some kinks, but as far as I'm concerned, this is a go. You'll leave for Seattle tomorrow morning. I'll have Clara send the details."

Ford let out a breath. "I can't believe that woman is good with making flights under aliases but still doesn't know we run black ops here."

Jett leveled him with a gaze, shutting off his laptop. "She thinks we're providing security. Traveling under a name other than our own isn't that far-fetched for providing protection. We're going under the radar to protect our clients."

Ford's lips quirked. "I'm guessing she suspects something. No one is that fucking naïve, not even her."

"Are we all set here, boss?" Luke asked. "I left a lady friend at my apartment. I'd love to get back before she up and bails."

Jett smirked but nodded. "We're done. I'll have the details sent over to you both," he said, eyeing Ford and Sam. "I'll let everyone know when Gray's starting. It'll be good to have a group of men we can trust."

"Harris was a dipshit," Nick said, referring to the man he'd let go. The bastard was lucky he hadn't ended up arrested. He'd certainly be on Jett's shitlist for life.

"He could've cost us a lot," Jett agreed. "Gray being here will be just like old times. Have a good Sunday afternoon, gentlemen. I left a beautiful lady at my own house and need to return."

The men's jaws dropped as Jett strode from the room. The team knew he never brought a woman home. Ever. They might as well get used to it. While he and Anna had danced around the idea of her staying longer than a single weekend, he wanted it to happen. He needed to see if what he was feeling was in any way real. He was too old for it to simply be hormones or the thrill of a new woman. It was her. Yes, he could admit he longed for her body, but her smile made him feel at peace. For a man that was always sure of himself, content to be alone, he almost wasn't sure what to make of this new development.

They needed to talk. She had to get back to Manhattan to clean out her desk and officially turn in her work credentials, but if he could convince her to stay with him? For real? Hell. She'd nonchalantly agreed this morning, but he needed her to know he was serious. Why get to know her while she was an hour away in the city? He wanted her here, in his home. In his life.

Jett strode out the front door of headquarters, whistling. He should pick up something on the way home for Anna. Flowers. Sexy lingerie. Both. They'd have dinner, spend some more quiet moments together, but he'd have to get her back by tomorrow morning, at least for a little while. He'd already stayed at the office longer than he'd intended. He'd ask Lena to purchase flowers and lingerie for Anna tomorrow. He'd already decided Anna would come back to his place. He'd surprise her then with some presents. And as for tonight? He'd make sure Anna knew he wanted her here longer than a single weekend.

Chapter 10

Anna gasped, arching atop Jett as she rode him. He'd woken her early this morning with soft kisses all over her body, and before long, he'd been claiming her once more. They were already on round two of their lovemaking, and Jett's big hands gripped her hips, guiding her. She might be on top this time, but he was still in control. His eyes were on her naked breasts as they bounced. He thrust his hips up as he rocked her against him. "Come for me," he ordered.

"Not yet," she said breathlessly.

Jett's thumb slid to her clit, stroking her. She faltered in her movements, sparks shooting through her entire body. This man was wicked. She wanted to feel his fullness longer, to savor this last moment of lovemaking before their magical weekend together really and truly came to an end.

"Come on, sweetness." Another thrust, and then he was expertly strumming her clit. His thick cock filled her as her inner walls clamped down around him. He thrust into her again. She reached the precipice, hanging there for an impossible moment, and then shattered, crying out as she collapsed on top of him.

Jett rolled them over in his massive bed, taking her faster. Harder. Her legs automatically wrapped around his waist. His lips caressed her neck. He finished with a groan as she clung to him, her pussy still spasming from her own orgasm. He shifted their bodies again so he didn't crush her.

"Oh God," she panted as his fingers ran through her hair. One hand palmed her ass, squeezing gently.

"Sweet Anna," he murmured. They lay there for a moment to catch their breaths, Anna draped over him. "I'm not ready to let you go. You'll come back to my place this afternoon?" he asked softly. They'd discussed it last night, but now it felt real. She could return to her old life in Manhattan or explore what this was between them.

"You're serious."

"Hell yes I'm serious. Should I make it clear by taking you again?"

She kissed his neck, lightly nipping at him, their bodies still joined together. "Yes. I'll pack a bag or two after I clear out my stuff from the office. I'll move in here for a little while, and we'll see what happens."

"Mmmm," he murmured. "I like the sound of that."

Jett rolled them to the side, so they were looking into one another's eyes. His cock slid from her pussy, causing them both to groan. "I meant what I said before. Stay as long as you want. I'll give you the keys to one of the cars so you can come and go. I'll have to work, of course, but—"

"I'll have to job hunt," she interrupted.

"About that. An idea occurred to me yesterday. What do you think about my offering you a job?"

"What?" she asked in surprise. "I'm not—"

"A job with Shadow Security," he hastily said, although she didn't miss the hungry way he looked down at her naked form. "Maybe I shouldn't have suggested it while you were naked in my bed. I could use someone to help run things in the office. My receptionist is a single mother who can't ever put in extra hours. Sometimes I have to go in on weekends, like yesterday, and I could use the additional help. I know she'd appreciate another person to help with the daily workload. I have an assistant, but she keeps my house and other affairs in order. This would be an administrative job, similar to what you do—what you did," he corrected. "I won't need you in the office at three a.m. or anything like that. This is mostly normal hours. Normal-ish."

"Wow. I don't know. I mean this—us—"

"Our relationship would be entirely separate from your employment." He grinned at her, looking devilishly sexy. "What can I say? I'm an unconventional man. I wasn't planning to offer you a job when I brought you home for the weekend, but if it works? Why not. You need a job. I need someone competent to help run the administrative side of things. Besides, I've been meaning to christen my office desk."

Anna burst into laughter, playfully swatting at him. Jett caught her hand, bringing it to his lips. He kissed it gently, the gesture sweet. "I'll think about it," she promised. "I will come stay with you for the week or however long we decide. I'm not sure about working for you."

"I want you here, Anna," he interrupted. "We've barely spent a moment apart all weekend, and I can't get enough of you. Yes, I'm attracted to you, but it's more than that."

"I feel it too," she admitted.

Jett wove his fingers between hers. "We'll even invite those friends of yours up here. Prove that I'm not some ax murderer, as you called it?"

She giggled. "A girl can't be too careful."

His eyes skimmed down her body. "You're all woman, sweetness. A woman I very much enjoy having in my life. I don't want to let you slip away."

She reached over and ran her free hand through his short, cropped hair, gazing into his eyes. The heat from Jett's large body radiated off him, and she was still flushed from their lovemaking. They were both relaxed and sated. The sincerity on his face was real though, and the butterflies in her stomach let her know this could be the start of something amazing. "Maybe I don't want you to slip away either."

"Then we're on the same page," he quipped. "I know I woke you up early, but we need to leave soon to get back given you have a job to officially quit this morning. Shower with me?"

"How will that help us to leave sooner?" she teased.

"We'll save time by showering together. And save water. Think of the environment," he added with a wink. Anna squealed as he suddenly stood, lifting her into his arms. Jett was still half-hard, but he strode across the master bedroom with her in his arms like a man on a mission. Who was she to stop him from getting what he wanted?

***

Several hours later, Anna was tossing clothes into her suitcase as she moved around the bed in her studio. Jett looked larger than life looming there watching her, but there wasn't much room in the cramped space.

"Are you serious?" Ashleigh asked on speakerphone. "You're moving in with Jett?"

"Yes, she's serious," he called out.

"Temporarily," Anna assured her friend. "I still have my studio. I'm just packing my bags to go stay with him for a while." She flinched as she heard her neighbors' bed knocking against the wall. Clearly, they didn't work normal nine-to-five jobs. Did they ever leave their actual bedroom? She didn't realize just how annoying they were because she was usually gone.

"So, when do I get to meet this guy?" Ashleigh pressed. "I know you have me on speaker. Jett, I've got to make sure you're not some serial killer or something. How do I know you're not going to bury her body in your backyard?"

Jett exchanged a glance with Anna, his lips quirking. "I run a security company. That'd be the first place they'd look if I needed to bury a body. Aren't you a writer? I bet you can come up with something better than that."

"Ha ha," Ashleigh muttered.

"We'd love to have you over this weekend," Jett continued. "I'll arrange for transportation if you ladies don't have cars. Jen can come, too. We'll make a night of it."

"See?" Anna asked. "He's inviting you both over. We'll have dinner and drinks. Relax. You can breathe in some fresh air and enjoy the stars. I'm not moving there forever, Ash, just seeing what happens. I know you think this is crazy, but just go with it."

"You're moving in with your one-night-stand. How is that not crazy?"

Anna shrugged. "You got me. You know I always do things my own way. So does Jett. It just makes sense given that I'm currently unemployed. If not now, when? I officially quit my job earlier—that was a long time coming, by the way. I packed up my desk and walked out of there. Of course, they asked me to put in my two weeks' notice, but I'd had enough."

"Well, I don't blame you for quitting that job, but—"

"You're happy for me that I met a nice guy? Thanks. You two are going to love each other. Maybe he's got a friend to set you up with."

"Anna!" she groaned. "I don't need you to set me up."

"I better finish packing. You know I've got lots of clothes, but I don't want to bring everything. Jett might rescind his invitation," she said, blowing him a kiss. "I promise everything will be fine, Ash. Let's talk soon."

"Yes, we absolutely will," Ashleigh pressed.

Anna said goodbye and hung up the phone, then flashed Jett a grin. "She's as bad as my mother. So, what do you think of my humble abode? You haven't said much since we got here."

Jett's eyes flicked around her small studio. "I understand this is what you could afford, but it doesn't suit you. I don't think the building's safe. The walls are thin. The locks could be stronger. The location is pretty decent; I'll give you that. Hell. I'm glad you're coming to stay with me."

Anna nodded toward his phone. "You've been getting a ton of texts. Are you missing out on something important by being here with me?"

"You're important."

"Okay, well, unlike me, I know you're still gainfully employed. Are you needing to do some work-related stuff? I know you've got a busy career running your own company and being the boss man."

"You could have a busy career, too. I've got plenty of work to offload on someone," he said with a wink.

"I don't think I could sleep with my boss," she countered.

"I own the whole company. I make the rules. The guys won't care. We served together in the Army. I've known them for years, and I'd trust them with my life. Believe me when I say this is the last thing they'd expect of me. We may have just met, Anna, but they'll know you're important to me if you're there."

She tilted her head, looking at him. "What exactly did you do in the Army? You said you were former military, but I don't know anything about your life back then. Not every man that leaves the service forms their own security company—or woman, I might add. I know women enlist as well."

He moved closer to her, his face serious. "The men who work for me were on my team," he said quietly. "Special Forces. I'll tell you more about it one day. Most things remain classified, but I don't mind sharing what I can. I gave ten years of service to my country. There was good and bad, just like anything in life."

"Special Forces, huh? I knew it. You are some super-secret bounty hunter."

"We do some classified work," he admitted. "But that's not public knowledge. Shadow Security offers protection to government officials and diplomats. We provide a variety of other services as well—things that aren't listed on my company website."

"Jett," she said hesitantly.

"I'll tell you what I can, Anna. I won't keep secrets from you if you're in my life. Promise me you'll at least consider my offer. We can discuss it more this week."

"When we're naked in bed?" she teased.

"Whenever you want," he said seriously. "You wouldn't ever be involved in anything dangerous. I do need admin help. You're quick-thinking and capable. Dedicated. It burns me up that you were in the office every weekend while your dick of a boss was fucking his mistress." His gaze scanned her small studio again.

Anna knew Jett didn't like that she lived here. It was safe enough. What could she do in an expensive city like Manhattan? She and Ashleigh had been roommates for several years, but she'd gotten to the point in her life where she enjoyed her own space. Funny she hadn't minded spending twenty-four/seven with Jett. They were new though—whatever "this" was. Maybe she'd go live with him and the little fairy tale they'd found themselves in would end. The bubble would burst. It was one thing to spend a romantic weekend together, connecting on every level, but about when real life crept in? They had jobs and the rest of the world to contend with.

"You're thinking too hard," he murmured.

"I'm considering your offer," she said, crossing to her lingerie drawer. "I need to think about it some." Anna yanked open the drawer, grabbing bras and panties, and suddenly Jett was interested in helping her pack. "Uh-uh. Hands off," she said, playfully swatting at him. "If you examine everything, we'll never get out of here."

"Good point. I'll examine them up close later on when you're wearing them."

"That's the spirit," she agreed. Jett's lips quirked, and he handed over the black lacy thong he was holding.

He cleared his throat. "There's an off-chance I may need to catch a flight later this week and meet with a contact. I'm waiting on confirmation."

"Wait. You're wanting me to move in with you this week and telling me you're leaving?"

"It's a possibility. It's work stuff. I could bring you along, sweetness, but I'm not sure that's the best idea. It's just a quick meeting, and you're a tempting distraction. It'll only be a day. I'll catch the red-eye back. You'll barely even miss me."

"Where are you going?" she asked, suddenly curious.

"Seattle."

"What? Well now I definitely want to come. Ashleigh is always talking about Seattle because her sister lives there. Can you believe I've never been? I'll buy a ticket and come, too."

"If you come with me, you're not buying a ticket, sweetheart. I'll pay for it."

"You can't keep paying for everything."

"I can, and I will. I own my company. I'm doing well. I know you work hard, but I'm older than you and established. It's not the same thing. If we travel together, I wouldn't ask for you to pay your own way."

"Well gosh, just keep spoiling me," she said with a wink.

He pulled her into his arms, letting his hands roam freely. She shivered at his touch. "I intend to. I'll admit I'm a man who works more than he plays, but I'm ready to change that. I do have a business to run, but I'd like to see what this is between us."

"This is crazy, isn't it?" she asked, looking up at him.

Jett ducked down for a kiss. "No. Not if we both feel the same way. Remember what I said the night we met? Maybe it's inevitable we'll be together."

"I didn't take you for such a romantic," she said, trying to hide her smile.

"I'm not. Never have been," he said with a chuckle. "I've also never felt this way about a woman before. If anyone told me I'd be head over heels after a couple of days, I'd think they were nuts."

"Head over heels, huh?" she asked, pressing closer.

Jett kissed the tip of her nose. "Be good, Anna. We have all night. You're moving in with me, remember?"

"Temporarily."

"Maybe we'll make it a permanent arrangement."

She giggled, rising up on her tiptoes to kiss him. Jett's hands wrapped around her waist, holding her close. She loved his strength and heat pressed against her. "Maybe. We'll play it by, ear, huh?" she asked.

"Woman, you've already got me wrapped around your finger."

"I'd rather be wrapped around you," she said sweetly.

Jett growled and pulled back. "Finish packing or we'll never get out of here. You're too damn tempting, Anna."

She turned away to stuff the last things into her suitcase but flashed him a look over her shoulder. "You're mighty tempting yourself."

Chapter 11

Jett strode into the office late that afternoon, a cup of coffee in his hand. He'd gotten Anna settled into his home for the most part, but work couldn't be avoided. Ford and Sam had landed in Seattle thirty minutes ago, and he'd gotten word from the Feds that the op was a go. Pacific Time was three hours behind Eastern Standard Time, so the men would have time to kill before the conference ended for the day. And then they'd keep eyes on Amir until the grab later this evening. Jett needed to confirm the pilot he paid a hefty sum to would be able to rendezvous at the scheduled time. McChord Field was about forty miles south of Seattle. The Air Force would allow Jett's chartered plane to land and take off. The military might not be running this op, but they would allow a small plane to land there as a favor to some higher-ups.

Jett smirked. He tried to avoid military installations

when he could. They didn't have a choice in this particular instance. While the men had flown commercial into the city, leaving with a diplomat was an entirely different beast. He didn't need records of the flight appearing on the books. Shadow Security tended to work overseas, but he didn't take issue with conducting missions on U.S. soil when needed.

And hell. A terrorist plotting against multiple large universities? They needed to know how far this network stretched. Students in the country on foreign visas were vetted before being allowed entry, but Amir could have radicalized them over the past year. Other threats could be on the horizon. The situation was a clusterfuck.

Clara looked up from the receptionist's desk as Jett came in, saying hello. "We've had several calls this morning about new clients seeking security services. I've forwarded the details to you to look over."

"Thank you, Clara," he said with a smile. "You always keep things running smoothly around here when I'm gone. As I mentioned, I had something to tend to earlier."

"It's no problem. Luke stopped in this morning and is working out, I believe, but it's been fairly quiet aside from the phone ringing."

"Ah. That reminds me. I know you're overworked with the increase in business we do here."

"Not at all, sir," she said, suddenly looking flustered.

"You're doing amazing," Jett reassured her, taking a sip of his coffee. "But I'd like to bring on additional admin staff. Sometimes the team and I convene on the weekends, and your hours are strictly Monday through Friday. We could use another hand."

"Your business is growing," she agreed.

"I've got a new hire as well for the security side. Gray Pierce. I'll be sending you some information to process for him. He's an old Army buddy of mine. He'll be a good addition to the team."

"No problem. I'll put through all the information once you send it over and get him whatever he needs."

"Excellent. With our workload, I might be hiring additional security staff in the future as well. Business is booming. We've got the space here, and I have the ability to bring on more men should the need arise. Having a support staff in place before that happens would be beneficial to all of us."

"It's grown a lot just since I've joined. Oh, and Lena stopped by, too. She said you wanted her to purchase some gifts?"

Jett chuckled, wondering what his assistant thought of his instructions. "Right. Did she drop them off? It's a surprise."

Clara smiled. "Yes. I set them back here. A wrapped present and some flowers."

"Perfect. I'll bring Anna in soon and introduce you ladies. She's the, uh, business I was tending to earlier. She'll be staying with me for the time being but also may be one of Shadow Security's new hires if I can convince her to work for me."

"Oh. Okay," Clara said, unable to completely conceal her surprise. "I can process her paperwork too when you're ready."

"Fantastic. Let me know if anything urgent arises. I'll be in my office," Jett said, heading back down the corridor. He typed in the code on the keypad to access the secure section of the building, the heavy door closing behind him. After moving down the hallway, Jett held his index finger to the scanner to open his own private office. The lights automatically came on as Jett entered the expensively furnished space. The large executive desk and built-in bookshelves held some of his materials. The table and leather chairs provided space for smaller meetings. Of course, much of the real work got done in the conference room with the entire team assembled. There was a state-of-the art gym on the other side of Shadow Security headquarters for the men to train. A gun range. Downstairs, behind secured doors, was the armory. Jett kept a stash of weapons, ammunition, and gear for their missions. The Shadow Ops Team had everything they needed at their disposal.

His receptionist knew about some of it. If the men were providing security, they needed weapons. The extent to what their operations involved wasn't something he'd divulged. Interestingly, Anna had already surmised that his work was dangerous. She was intelligent. Observant. If she did become his, he'd have to share some of what his company really did. He'd never discuss specifics, of course, in order to ensure her safety. He'd have to fill her in on the fact that he ran a black ops team. He was shocked at his line of thinking. Jett had known her for mere days, and he was already considering the possibility of a future with her.

He also knew their connection wasn't something that just happened. In an odd way, he was more comfortable with Anna than alone. She completed him in a way he didn't fully understand. Calmed his thoughts. Made him feel grounded. Nothing had been missing from his life before, or maybe he'd just been too damn busy to notice. Now that she was here in his life, it was hard to imagine letting her go.

Jett logged in to his computer and read through some of his emails. Often times meeting in person was preferable to discuss the finite details. The government didn't want records, electronic or otherwise, to what his team was tasked to do. Jett kept files here, but there was nothing tying him to the agencies he worked with.

He clicked on another message, frowning as he saw his contact in Seattle did want to meet this week. The DOD higher up was there attending a separate conference and would be flying to Asia shortly afterward. How about that for timing. The world was a damn big place, and here Jett would be flying into Seattle shortly after his team was flying out.

Jett clenched his hands together, stretching his arms. It wouldn't be the worst thing in the world to bring Anna along. He'd meet with his contact to determine if Shadow Security would take the mission, and then he and Anna could enjoy the day in Seattle. He'd met with a contact before he'd approached Anna at the bar in Manhattan on Friday evening. This wasn't all that different. Sam and Ford would confirm when their separate operation was complete. If trouble arose, he'd be there to smooth things over. While he'd originally planned to catch the red-eye back, they could spend the night there.

He drummed his fingers on the desk. There was already another op looming overseas, potentially rescuing several American women who'd been trafficked. The government didn't want to send in the military due to diplomatic relations. An off-the-books mission would allow for rescue of the women and keep the government's hands from getting dirty. This meeting in Seattle was simple. Cut and dry. There wasn't a reason not to bring Anna along on this quick trip. Swiping the screen on his cell phone, he called her.

"Miss me already?" she asked. "It's barely been an hour since you left."

"Of course I miss you," he said with a low chuckle. "How's unpacking coming along?"

"Great. Your closet is massive. I think it might be the size of my entire studio apartment. I might just stay forever simply because of the closet space. That kind of square footage doesn't come along every day."

He smiled, loving the playful banter between them. "So, you're using me just because you like things…big?"

"You know it," she teased.

"I do my best to please," he said huskily. "Are you still interested in a trip to Seattle with me this week?"

"Seriously?" she asked with a laugh. "I was giving you a hard time earlier, but sure. I figure I deserve a few days to unwind and figure out what I want to do with my life. Then it'll be time to hunker down and job hunt—or think about your offer."

"I already let my receptionist know we might be bringing you onboard."

"You did not."

"I did," he said, a smile tugging at his lips. "I can be very persuasive when I want to be."

"That you can be, but so can I. Maybe you've met your match and just don't realize it yet."

He burst into laughter. "I very much doubt that, sweetness. Not that I'm opposed to letting you try.

I've got to work here a few hours since I was out all morning but thought we could cook dinner together later."

"You need me to help you cook?" she asked. He could picture her smiling.

"I'll run out of recipes I know soon if I'm left completely to my own devices. Normally Lena leaves some prepared meals in the fridge for me. I work crazy hours sometimes, but I'll keep it to a minimum this first week while you're settling in. I want to spend time with you."

"Cooking dinner together sounds great. I'm already in love with your kitchen. You saw the ridiculous kitchen space in my studio."

He made a noise of disapproval. Jett knew she lived where she could afford. That was better than going into debt over rent, but damn. He didn't want to send her back there. "That I did, and as you already know, I much prefer having you here. I'll have my staff book us tickets to Seattle. And you're all set with the alarms at the house in case you need to leave?"

"I think so. I'm not planning to run any errands this afternoon though. Honestly, I'm a little overwhelmed with quitting my job and then rushing with you up here. I need the afternoon just to decompress."

He frowned. "I don't want you to feel pressured to stay with me."

"I don't. Not at all. This weekend was amazing. I'm just a little out of sorts since I'm not used to sitting around on a Monday afternoon. It's weird. Some of my coworkers were texting me, asking what happened. I didn't even give two weeks' notice. I just up and quit. My boss calling me on Saturday night was probably for the best. I've been meaning to quit and search for something better, and I finally did it. Go me."

Jett chuckled. "All right, as long as you're not regretting this."

"Not at all. Of course, Ashleigh texted me again asking if I'd completely lost my mind. I told her she needed to have great sex more often, then she'd get it," Anna teased. "And I bet a man has never served her breakfast in bed either."

"It was my pleasure," he said huskily. "I really do have to finish up here. I'll be home around six."

"Sounds good, baby," she teased. "Maybe I'll be waiting in a silk robe and sexy lingerie."

"Anna," he growled.

"See you then!" She ended the call, leaving Jett's blood heating at the thought. Lena knew not to suddenly stop by with Anna there, but hell. Now he'd have thoughts of Anna running through his head all afternoon. He'd asked Lena to purchase Anna some lingerie anyway. Next time he'd pick it out himself. He liked the idea of coming home and spoiling her. Flowers. Lingerie. He'd have to come up with some other ideas in the future. Did she like reading? Art? Music?

Jett knew they still had a lot to learn about one another. That didn't stop the way she always made him smile. He scrubbed a hand over his jaw. Anna was the best sort of trouble, but he needed to focus on his work this afternoon, not be caught up thinking about the tempting woman at home.

Chapter 12

The phone buzzing on his nightstand woke Jett from a deep sleep at three a.m. Muttering a curse, he silenced it and stood, untangling himself from the covers. Jett walked swiftly across the master bedroom. The moonlight lit a dim path, and he quietly headed toward the hallway. Anna was asleep in his bed, the black lacy negligee he'd gotten her discarded on the floor. The flowers were in a vase on the nightstand, save for the one rose he'd used to explore and tease her body. Jett had blindfolded her, running the soft petals over her breasts and nipples, tracing it across her stomach. She'd squirmed beneath him as he'd kissed her inner thighs, and then he'd pleasured her, kissing and licking her soft folds until she was begging him to let her come.

Anna thought she was a match for him? It was amusing to watch, not to mention arousing as hell when she tried to gain the upper hand. He loved being in control, and having a woman like her pleading to come made him thrill at the challenge. He'd wanted to roar in approval as she'd finally cried out her pleasure in his bed, at Jett's complete and utter mercy. They'd made love slowly afterwards, with Anna falling asleep in his arms when they were both thoroughly sated.

This phone call was a far cry from his romantic evening, however. Ford and Sam shouldn't have completed the mission yet. It was only midnight Seattle time, and Amir was known to visit nightclubs until the early morning hours. It was unlikely they'd call unless there was a problem. "Jett here," he said in a low voice as the bedroom door clicked shut. He strode down the hallway in his boxers, moving toward his home office.

"We've got a problem, boss," Ford said. "Amir didn't venture out to the nightclub he's been going to all week."

"What? Where is he?" Jett asked with a frown.

"Still at the hotel where the conference is being held. He was with a woman."

"Fuck," Jett muttered. "Amir never left the hotel tonight?"

"Affirmative. He's still in the building. Breaching his room—or her room, as the case may be—with both of them inside would be a distraction we can't afford. There are cameras in the halls, witnesses. We're waiting to see if he leaves. We could pull the fire alarm, but then we'd have to find him in the crowd. With police and emergency crews at the scene, it would draw that much more attention to the place."

"Damn it," Jett muttered. "He's been at that club every other night during the conference. I knew we should've gone in, but the Feds were moving too damn slowly to authorize this. I want him before he flies back to D.C. I'll contact the pilot and let him know we might not be going wheel's up at the prearranged hour. We'll have to coordinate with the Feds as well since they'll be waiting for the package."

"Roger that, boss."

"Keep me posted. We'll move to Plan B if needed." Jett ended the call and grabbed a burner phone to send a text to his contact.

Silent night.

They had personnel on standby at the black ops site for Amir's arrival, except he was still in fucking Seattle. Jett scrubbed a hand over his jaw. He'd wanted to send in a team earlier this weekend, but they were awaiting the go. If the Feds were paying Shadow Security, they called the shots on authorization to move forward. Plus, Jett needed to make use of the military airfield for this mission. Hell. This was a complication he didn't need, especially if he'd be sending other men in after the trafficked women soon on a separate operation. He needed a second Shadow Ops Team at this rate. They were already being stretched too damn thin.

His phone buzzed with a text.

Roger. We're ready for Christmas here.

They were assembled, and Amir was with a woman. Of course. Wasn't that the problem with most of the male population? A single woman could bring a man to his knees, making him lose all sense. Their last operative had fucked up because of a tempting female. Now their target was thinking with his dick, too. He didn't have any female operatives to tempt Amir—not that one could innocuously barge into the hotel room either.

A soft knock on his office door had Jett looking up. "Come in," he said quietly.

Anna padded in, rubbing sleep from her eyes. She'd pulled one of his tee shirts on instead of her own clothing, and his need flared. Her breasts pressed against the soft cotton, and he could see her nipples through the fabric. The shirt was long on her, hitting her thighs, but he knew her pussy would be bare beneath. Maybe it was rather caveman-ish of him, but he loved seeing her in his clothes. Loved looking at her.

"Is everything okay?" she asked, yawning.

Jett nodded, drawing her into his arms. Anna came willingly and nestled against him like she belonged there. She still smelled like those damn peaches and was soft and warm curled against his muscular frame. "Yep. Just work stuff. Sorry if I woke you. I closed the office door to keep quiet."

"I'm a light sleeper," she confessed. "It made for long nights in the city that never sleeps."

"I'll bet," he said, trailing a hand through her hair. Her bare legs tangled between his own, but at the moment he just felt content holding her. He already felt more settled now that she was here in his arms. He still had his op to deal with, but she soothed him somehow. Calmed his frayed nerves. "I need to do some research, but then I'll come back to bed. I need to update my men on something."

"Research at three in the morning?" she asked warily.

"Sweetness, you know my company does a variety of work. Some of my guys are gone, and I need to check into something. Just making sure everything goes smoothly from here on out."

"Need help?" she asked.

He stilled. Anna would help him if he asked. This type of thing wasn't appropriate though. Looking into a suspected terrorist wasn't following his plans of keeping her safe. "Not this time. And if you did work for me, I wouldn't have you doing anything that would put you at risk."

Anna leaned back, looking up at him. "Just what kind of risky research are you doing in the middle of the night?"

He met her gaze. "Researching someone we're monitoring. I can't go into details."

"But you trust me enough to offer me a job?" she asked.

Jett let out a sigh. "All right, sweetness. Confession time. The night we met, I ran a background check on you." Jett was surprised as Anna burst into laughter, her small body shaking against his own. "I thought you'd be mad," he admitted.

"You run a security company. I'd have to be naïve if I thought you didn't look into a single thing about me. I texted my friends your driver's license, remember? It's not the same, but they absolutely googled you and scoured social media to see what they could find."

"Fair enough," he said with a smile. "Did I pass the test?"

"You must have. If not, you better believe Ashleigh would've had the police or FBI knocking at your door. She would've gotten them to drag my ass back to the city."

His lips quirked. "You passed as well, Anna. You've never had so much as a speeding ticket. I can't have you dealing with some stuff my company is involved in. It's too dangerous. We work with the government, but my team consists of former Special Forces soldiers. Admin stuff is one thing, but I want to keep you safe."

She lifted a slender hand, running it over the stubble on his jaw. "And I like that about you. I mean, sure, I love teasing you, but I like that you're concerned about me. It's sweet."

"I'm not sweet," he grumbled.

"You brought me flowers."

"And then ran the petals over your naked body," he said, his cock twitching at the memory.

She smiled but slid off his lap. "And then you made love to me all soft and gentle after that. You're assertive, yes, but you're sweet, too. Don't try to deny it. I'm not sure I even want to know what dangerous stuff you're dealing with in the middle of the night anyway. I'm going back to sleep because I'm tired, but my offer stands if you ever truly need my help. Come back to bed soon?"

"With you in my bed? Absolutely."

Jett stood up and pulled her close, kissing her softly. It was intimate to kiss a woman like this at three in the morning. They weren't about to rip each other's minimal clothes off again. It was a kiss saying he cared about her. It was too soon for love—far too soon for that. But the feelings he had were growing stronger. Jett never believed in love at first sight or soulmates or any of that nonsense. He couldn't deny the sense of peace he had around Anna though. Was it too good to be true? Time would tell. His gut told him it was the start of something incredible.

Chapter 13

"Wake up, sweetness," Jett murmured at oh-five-hundred the next morning. He hadn't gone back to bed after all, instead standing by for further updates from Ford. Amir had never left the damn hotel, which fucked up all their plans.

Ford and Sam were implementing Plan B. One of the men would lie in wait in Amir's own hotel room, incapacitating him when he returned to get ready for the day. Breaching the empty room had been easy. There was no need to worry about someone inside screaming and alerting the authorities. No one was there to dial 911. They just needed Amir to return to his own hotel for the shock of his lifetime.

The men wouldn't risk removing Amir in broad daylight; they'd hold him there until nightfall. When it was safe to slip out under the cover of darkness, they'd head to McChord Field. Waiting around Amir's hotel all day with him in captivity wasn't ideal. Hotel staff or housekeeping could come in. Amir's own staff could attempt contact. It was a risk, but one that they'd need to take in order to exfiltrate him. With the conference ending tomorrow, he'd be flying back to D.C. Jett already had their next mission on his radar. This operation needed to be completed ASAP. The Feds needed to question Amir and prevent any attacks on American universities. If he claimed diplomatic immunity and left the country on his own, the entire situation would be a clusterfuck.

There were always other missions looming on the horizon. Terrorists to take out. Hostages to secure rescue of. Jett's team would handle the instances the government wouldn't send in the military for. Not every situation was cut and dry, and they'd deal with the aftermath. The government might fund them, but without the U.S. operating in foreign countries in an official capacity on these missions, they'd be clean.

If Jett or his men were ever caught while on foreign soil? They'd be on their own. The dangers of his career were very real. All of his men were single, without the complications having a serious girlfriend or wife entailed. That had never bothered Jett until now. The woman in his bed was someone special. If Anna were to up and leave, despite the short amount of time they'd known one another, it would be a loss. She filled a need he didn't even realize he had—a part of him he hadn't even known was empty.

Hell. He didn't even know what she wanted in life. Anna was young. Was she hoping for kids and a family? A white picket fence in the suburbs? His career was risky. He was a busy man. That didn't mean he didn't want to give them a chance to be together.

Jett gently brushed her hair back from her face, murmuring to her again. Anna finally stirred, blinking as she looked up at him. She'd kept his tee shirt on, and he wanted to roar in approval. Seeing her in his bed, in his clothes…. She was his. That was all that mattered.

"What time is it?" she asked, her voice heavy with sleep.

"Early. I've got to head into the office to deal with some stuff. I didn't want to leave without letting you know. I might bring one of the guys around later to introduce you. Since you'll be staying here, I'd like for you to meet my team."

"Mmmm, okay. That's a good idea."

"I'll let you know before we come, but make sure you're decent." He winked, and she playfully pouted at him.

Jett's gaze roamed over her body. "No one else needs to see what's mine," he said roughly.

"You never came back to bed. Were you up all night?" she asked.

He nodded. "Some of my men are gone on a job, so I was monitoring things. I need to head in though to deal with a complication."

"With the person you were watching," she said astutely.

Jett wasn't surprised she remembered their conversation in the middle of the night. Anna was sharp. "Yes. I shouldn't be gone too long, but you have my number if you need something. Later this week, maybe after Seattle, I'll bring you into the office. I want to show you around headquarters and introduce you to some more people."

"Are they going to try to talk me into working for

Shadow Security, too?" she teased.

"If they know what's good for them," he said, ducking down to brush a kiss against her forehead. Her hair was sexily disheveled from last night, and he wished he didn't have to leave her here in his bed. Work couldn't be avoided though. If he and Anna were ever to really be together, she'd have to realize that emergencies came up. Not every op ran smoothly. She didn't look upset though, which boded well for them. He liked that she was independent.

"Miss you," she said sleepily.

Jett smiled. "I'll miss you, too, sweetness." He stood and turned, heading to the bathroom to quickly shower. He was already half-hard just from looking at her. Getting the mission back on track was critical. If that fucker Amir didn't return to his hotel this morning, they'd need other plans in place to secure him. Naturally he'd diverted from his pattern the night they were to grab him. Shit was about to hit the fan, and they needed to get him before that happened.

***

"What's up, boss?" Nick asked as Jett stormed into the conference room. He was already seated at the table, arms crossed, a cup of coffee in front of him. "I rolled my ass out of bed crazy early to get here ASAP."

"Sam and Ford are still in Seattle," Jett said in a clipped tone. He dropped his files down on the table.

"Shit," Nick said, scrubbing a hand over his jaw.

"Shit is right. Amir was with a woman last night. He never even went to the nightclub. He's been in some lady's room since yesterday evening when the conference ended for the day. They weren't able to grab him."

"Damn. Guess that plan is FUBAR," Nick said. "What's next?"

Jett met Nick's gaze. His men rolled with the punches and were ready to move on to Plan B, C, and D if needed. They'd had multiple back-up plans while in the Special Forces and still operated the same way now. Quick thinking allowed them to complete their missions no matter what obstacles were thrown in their path. It was a skill honed over years in the Army but served them well today. He appreciated that Nick was already thinking ahead toward their next move.

"Ford is waiting in Amir's hotel room to ambush him. He'll need to go back to shower and change before the sessions begin today. He had his briefcase last night but went upstairs with a woman. There was no suitcase or overnight bag."

"Wasn't he with someone else earlier this week?" Nick asked.

"Yes, and our sources indicate there was a third woman he was bedding as well. It's a large conference with academics from all over the country. He's made himself known in those circles, no doubt trying to get information about the campus and students. He enjoys women, and Amir is a wealthy man."

"He's buying them off with expensive gifts and shit?"

"It's possible. I don't know if he's hoping to get access to buildings on campus or what. Maybe he's gathering information. We've been concerned with the recruitment of university students for his terror plot, but this is another dimension worth exploring. The Feds no doubt have an extensive list of questions for him. We just need to deliver the damn package."

"Why is he staying in a different hotel than where the conference is being held?"

"He's paying for a luxury suite at a more expensive place."

"Figures. The man's got money," Nick said.

Jett's phone buzzed, and he glanced down to read the text. "Amir still hasn't shown up at his hotel."

Nick frowned. "It's early there with the three-hour time difference. Maybe he wanted another roll in the sack before getting ready. Are we sure he's heading back there?"

"Nothing's certain," Jett said. "Ford is waiting in his room, but Sam's got eyes in the lobby. He'll see if Amir leaves. We need to go over alternate scenarios for exfiltration. Aside from the conference tomorrow, my pilot is only on standby for so long. He'll be there tonight, but if Amir doesn't show this morning, we need a new plan to grab him."

Luke came walking into the conference room, his blue eyes alert as he caught the end of the conversation. "I'm guessing last night was a wash."

Jett briefly brought Luke up to speed. "When's his flight back to D.C.?" Luke asked. "Maybe they can grab him on the way to the airport."

"It's possible but risky. He's set to fly out tomorrow when the conference ends, but it will still be broad daylight. It'd be one thing if he was going to be alone in a dark parking garage. He'll have a cab or private driver. It's probably already been arranged. If we wait until tomorrow to grab Amir, I'll need a new pilot and plane at McChord Field."

"Well shit. Maybe a fake woman can ask him to rendezvous at his own hotel room," Luke said. "We'll lure him in, but Ford and Sam will be waiting."

"It's a possibility, but let's go over all alternate scenarios for extraction," Jett said. "Luke, look over the hotel schematics where the conference is being held. If Amir doesn't leave the building today, we can look into ways of isolating and grabbing him there. Sam and Ford also have copies of the blueprint for the luxury hotel where he's staying, but those are two separate places. Let's consider all options."

"What about an emergency?" Nick said. "They can trash his hotel room and call in a burglary. Amir will be forced to return, but they can grab him before he gets back."

"That'd bring a lot of unwanted attention to Amir. Taking him at night at least provided the possibility of an anonymous robbery or carjacking. The Feds aren't telling the local police about this. Hell. We're trying to avoid causing a ruckus."

"All right. What about dinner?" Nick asked. "We'll find out where he's eating later on, and they'll grab him in the alley."

Jett drummed his fingers on the table. "List all possibilities. Everything. We'll brainstorm options if our plans already in place fall through. If he doesn't show this morning, they'll take him by other means."

Chapter 14

Anna sat at Jett's kitchen table that afternoon, mindlessly searching for jobs on her laptop. He'd been gone for hours, and although she had plenty of ways to entertain herself, she felt restless. It was strange to be home once again in the afternoon while everyone she knew was at work. Her coworkers were no doubt slammed. Ashleigh would be busy writing. Jen would be at her office. Even Jett, her one-night-stand turned sort-of boyfriend, was busy with his job. He was meeting with his men.

She was just...restless. Anna blew out a sigh. Jumping back into the craziness of Manhattan wasn't necessarily what she wanted. Hadn't she told Jett that she'd discovered city life wasn't for her? She couldn't just stay here doing nothing though. Maybe for a week or so while she figured stuff out, but certainly not forever. Jett had sensed that, she supposed. He'd offered her a job because he said he wanted her to stay. It'd be crazy to accept his offer though, wouldn't it?

Maybe no crazier than diving back in to a life she didn't love in Manhattan.

Standing up, she walked into his living room, looking at the photos on the wall she'd seen the first night. Jett looked handsome in his uniform. Young, too. Not that he looked especially old now, but he'd certainly had more of an innocence about him then in his early military days. Jett was a hardened warrior. He was gruff and assertive, but she loved that he could also be gentle with her. She scanned the faces of some of the other men in the pictures, wondering if they were the men he worked with now.

Anna wandered further down the hallway. His office was filled with military books, nonfiction, and a couple of spy novels thrown in. She smiled. He didn't seem like the type of man to sit around idly reading. At his house, they'd spent nearly every waking moment together. He had more personal pictures here in his office: a photo of him and his brother rock climbing, an old family photograph. There were no pictures of ex-girlfriends, but then again, he'd said he didn't really have time to date.

Shaking her head, Anna wandered back into the kitchen. Although Jett had offered her his office to set up her laptop, it felt strange, like she was intruding somehow. She'd slipped into his life, but where did that leave her? She had a suitcase full of clothes here and a few personal things. That was all. Anna clicked through some other executive assistant positions being advertised. She wasn't hurting for money, but she wouldn't just mooch off of Jett. Her stomach sank as she read some of the job descriptions—

overtime, bonus pay. She'd be jumping right back into the life she'd already had.

Glancing down at her phone, she realized Jett had texted her ten minutes ago to say he'd be back soon. She wrinkled her brow in confusion as she heard the front door open. Why hadn't he parked in the garage?

"Knock-knock," a deep, male voice said as someone walked into Jett's house. Someone who was definitely not him. And apparently, he had a key. She wasn't scared, exactly, just surprised. Jett had alarms in his house. Fences surrounding the property. A gate out front. Yet this man clearly knew how to get inside.

"Sorry if I scared you," a large, muscular man said as he walked into the kitchen. He hesitated in the doorway, seemingly not wanting to frighten her further. "I would've knocked, but that sets off the damn alarm sometimes. Jett said earlier that he hadn't shown you how to access the camera feeds at the gate yet. I'm Luke Willard. I work for Jett."

"One of his Army friends I assume," Anna said, standing up. "I'm Anna Dubois." The large man crossed the kitchen to shake her hand. He was as big as Jett, maybe a few years younger. She was barefoot, so she felt even smaller beside him. She wasn't uncomfortable, necessarily, just aware of his size and strength.

"Guilty as charged," Luke said, his gaze briefly flicking to her laptop. "We served together, and now I work for Shadow Security. Jett's picking up some things but wanted me to meet you this afternoon. We've been working all morning, as he probably told you. I actually thought we'd get here at the same time," he said with an easy smile.

"Nope. It's just me. I know you said knocking could trigger the alarm, but doesn't Jett have a doorbell?" she asked quizzically.

"He does, but it rings to the software on his phone."

"Oh," Anna said. "Why doesn't he want the doorbell to ring inside the house?"

Luke lifted a shoulder. "Most people have to access the front gate anyway, so there's not really a need. If they show up at his front door, he already knows that they're here. The team and I have the codes."

"Right."

Luke crossed Jett's kitchen and opened the fridge, pulling out a bottle of water. "We were surprised when he said you were staying with him. I guess there's a first time for everything."

"What do you mean?" Anna asked, watching as Luke unscrewed the bottle cap and took a swig. She wondered where all the men trained. Jett was muscular and fit. She'd seen a treadmill here in his home, but the muscles that both Jett and Luke had came from lifting weights and strength training.

"I don't think he's ever brought a woman here. His assistant Lena comes by, of course, but a woman he's seeing? That's a negative."

"Huh," Anna said as she mulled that over. Things had progressed so smoothly on Friday, she'd kind of assumed Jett did that sort of thing all the time. He'd picked her up at a bar, invited her to his home. Then again, she didn't ever go home with a strange man she'd just met. They'd just looked at one another across that crowded bar and connected. It was cliché and a little bit crazy. Oddly enough, it made her feel better knowing Jett never did this either. He'd told her he didn't date, but she didn't think Luke would randomly bring it up if it weren't true.

Luke's lips pulled into a smile. "I'm serious. He never really dates much. We're busy with work, so none of the guys have serious girlfriends or anything like that. But to have you stay with him? We were joking this weekend that we'd be expecting wedding invitations soon."

"No," she said with a laugh. "Nothing like that."

Luke's gaze slid to her laptop again. "Are you job hunting? The boss gave me the impression you'd be coming onboard at Shadow Security."

Just then, Jett came walking into the kitchen himself, muttering under his breath as he glared at Luke. "I thought you'd wait for me to get here. Did this idiot scare you half to death?" he asked, his eyes sweeping toward Anna.

"No. Startled, maybe, but I figured not just anyone could get into your house."

Jett set the bag he was carrying down on the counter, crossing over to wrap his arm around Anna's shoulders. He leaned down and kissed her temple. "Sorry. I'll inform my men that they're not to barge in here."

"Oh, it's okay," Anna said, noticing the concern in Jett's eyes. He'd been up for much of the night and still seemed a bit stressed now. Maybe Jett was more worried about her at the moment than whatever work stuff he was dealing with. He was protective of her. She liked that he wanted to make sure she felt safe in his house. "Seriously, it's fine."

Jett's dark gaze flicked over to Luke, who had the decency to look a bit chagrined. "It won't happen again, boss. I figured you'd be here already."

Jett blew out a sigh. "It took longer than expected. Anna, you've already met Luke Willard I take it. I'll introduce you to the rest of my men so you'll know the entire team. We do meet here sometimes, so you'll get to know them. Usually I have Lena arrange everything. These guys would eat me out of house and home without her planning for food and drinks," he joked.

"I can help if I'm here," Anna said.

"If you'd like, but there's no need for you to feel obligated. I pay my assistant to handle those details."

"You could join in when the shop talk is done," Luke said, eyeing them with amusement. Anna didn't miss the way his gaze flicked between Jett and her.

"Maybe if it's a dinner or something," she said. "I don't need to crash a work-related meeting."

"We'd be good," Luke assured her.

Anna laughed, glancing up at Jett. "Somehow I very much doubt that."

"I like her," Luke said, taking another swig of his water. "Let me know if you have any single friends, Anna," he added with a wink. Jett growled slightly as Luke chuckled. "I'll let you two lovebirds play house or whatever. The boss is getting ticked at me. Nice to meet you, Anna."

"Likewise."

"I'll walk you out," Jett said, crossing the kitchen to escort Luke out of his home. "Don't come in here again without knocking." He said something else that she didn't quite catch, and then Anna heard the front door close and lock. A moment later, Jett came back into the kitchen.

"How'd you know he let himself in?" she asked.

"Security cameras."

"Oh. Right. I'm not used to all that stuff. My studio has locks and a peephole to look through but that's about it. He did surprise me, but I figured it was one of your friends since you'd said you wanted us to meet."

"I'm sorry about that," Jett murmured as he pulled her close. "I'm damn sure he did that on purpose just to see you without me around."

She giggled, clutching onto him. "Are you jealous?"

"No, because you're sleeping in my bed at night. I still don't want those idiots to scare you by coming in unannounced. I already spoke with Lena about it. I didn't think to spell it out for those knuckleheads who work for me. I'll show you how all the security cameras work and inform my team to identify themselves at the gate. It won't happen again."

"I think he was sorry," Anna said soothingly.

Jett eyed her. "I want you to feel safe here." He ducked down and kissed her softly, and Anna felt shivers racing down her spine. She clung to Jett's shirt as she looked up at him. As unsettled as she'd been this afternoon, just seeing him made her feel like it was the right decision to be here. Jett made her feel safe. Secure. Yes, he had a demanding career, but he'd been worrying about her. "I'm sorry I was gone for so much of the day," he said huskily. "Things weren't going as planned, so my team and I had to work the issue."

"Oh," she said, her face falling.

Jett ran one big hand through her hair, his fingers tangling in her tresses. "We'll figure it out. Are you still up for coming to Seattle with me tomorrow?"

She shrugged. "I'm fine with that. No job, remember?"

His lips quirked. "We can change that."

Anna's gaze slid to the counter, eyeing the bag he'd brought in. "You went grocery shopping?"

Jett pulled away and crossed over to it, letting her change the subject. "I picked up a few things. We'll have dinner later on and pack. I need to put some of this in the fridge."

Anna went over to help him as Jett's phone buzzed. He frowned as he read the text, but she pulled out the food from the grocery bag: wine, ravioli, pasta sauce, a salad kit, and shredded parmesan. She began putting things away, smiling as she caught him watching her. "What?"

His lips quirked. "I like having you here. It won't always be like this, I know. We'll be at work and rushing home to eat. If you end up turning down my offer and working in the city, well, it might just be weekends that we're together. But cutting out early to spend an afternoon with you isn't a hardship. I need to call Clara and have her book our flights. We'll leave early in the morning."

"What about that work problem you're dealing with?"

"The guys will keep me updated. Right now, I just need to wait and see how it all plays out. I can't discuss the details, sweetness."

She bit her lip, worry flooding through her. It was weird. She didn't know the first thing about what he was dealing with, but for some reason, an ominous feeling washed over her. His work didn't involve her in any way, but she couldn't help but worry. "It's all right," Jett soothed, moving closer as he sensed her concern. He pulled her into his arms, and then his lips found her neck, kissing her softly. Anna gasped and clung to him, her body heating at his touch.

"Maybe I'll call her later," Jett said huskily. Without another word, he lifted Anna into his arms. She shrieked in surprise, but then Jett's lips were on hers as he carried her down the hallway to his bedroom.

Chapter 15

The sound of the alarm at four in the morning had Anna groaning and pulling the pillow down over her head. Jett shut off the blaring noise and then pulled her to him with a low chuckle. "Good morning."

"Morning?" she mumbled. "It's more like the middle of the night."

"If you want to come to Seattle with me, we've got to get ready."

"It's so early. Are you sure you can't just have a phone conversation with this person you're meeting?"

"Not about this, sweetness."

She mumbled a response into the pillow as Jett stroked her back. He'd been up for hours last night dealing with the clusterfuck of a mission. Amir was in the wind. He'd never returned to his luxury hotel at all yesterday. He'd skipped out on the conference. Sam had eventually searched the room of the woman Amir had spent the night with, but there were no traces of him.

Had he somehow gotten wind of the operation? Ford had breached his hotel room in the early morning hours. It was possible someone had informed Amir of the incident. Maybe he'd put hidden cameras in his room to keep an eye on his belongings or for some other nefarious purpose. None of it made sense. Jett had gotten one of his IT gurus to hack into the security cameras of the conference hotel. There was no sign of Amir leaving the building. The diplomat had a flight out of Seattle this evening, heading back to D.C. His men would have eyes on both hotels today but otherwise would plan to be at the airport this evening to see if he showed. Jett would join them himself if he had to. They'd also be tracking him by other means—credit card usage, cell phone signals. It was unlikely he'd show for the final day of the conference, but they'd know if he did.

Luke and Nick would be at headquarters, monitoring things. They'd find another pilot on Jett's extensive list of contacts. One way or another, they'd get Amir tonight.

"Okay, well, who am I to be the voice of reason here?" Anna said into the pillow. "You say you've got this meeting with someone. Will you still have time to spend with me?"

He smiled. "I will. Our meeting will be brief. I do have a separate issue to deal with, but my team is on it. Hopefully they won't need me at all. You can relax at the hotel or do a little sightseeing on your own. We'll have the rest of the day to explore the city, plus tomorrow before we fly back. With the time difference, the flight today will have us arriving not long after we left," he said with a chuckle. "We'll catch some of the highlights of Seattle. Another time, we'll go away for a long weekend together."

"Back to Seattle?" she asked.

"Anywhere you want. Paris. London."

"Ohhh, I like the sound of Paris."

"Then it's a done deal. I may have mentioned that I plan to spoil you," he said huskily, ducking down to kiss her bare shoulder. "I intend to make good on my promise."

She yanked the pillow off her head and smiled up at him, their eyes locking for a moment. He did want to spoil this woman—travel with her everywhere. See the world. The traveling he'd done in the past was mostly with the military or on black ops missions. Playing tourist would be a new one for him, but Jett wasn't opposed to the idea. He'd take Anna wherever she wanted.

"Okay. I'm up for a quick Seattle trip," she said, sitting up in bed. The covers fell away from her, revealing her naked form. Jett had to resist reaching out and caressing her bare breasts. Kissing her everywhere. He'd love to spend a leisurely morning in bed, but they did need to get ready.

"Let's shower together," he said, taking her hand and standing. He guided her to the master bathroom, turning on the water.

"Did I tell you I had more texts about quitting my job? No one can believe it," she said. Despite himself, Jett's lips quirked. Only Anna would stand here naked discussing her job like it was a perfectly normal thing to do. Damn. He was falling for this woman. She wasn't shy in the least, and he loved how comfortable she was in her own skin.

"Your former boss was a fool," Jett said, ducking down for a kiss. He clasped her hands, weaving his fingers between hers.

"Yeah, well, one of the texts was from him. He offered to double my salary."

"I'll triple it," Jett immediately said.

"You don't even know what I made," Anna said with a laugh. "What if I'm a terrible employee who can't get anything right? Maybe I hit 'reply all' to every email and bombard the office with spam and invitations to my multi-level marketing parties."

Jett raised an eyebrow. "What the hell is that?"

She giggled. "Those sales parties. You host something and invite friends over but secretly just want them to purchase candles and things."

Jett's deep laughter echoed throughout the bathroom as he guided her into the shower. "I promise you none of my guys would want to buy candles."

Anna playfully nudged him, the warm water dampening her hair and running over her bare skin. "I know, I'm just saying you're awfully confident in offering me a job. We still don't know everything about each other."

He leveled her with a gaze, backing her against the tile wall. His arms landed on either side of her head, effectively caging her in. Anna smiled, her expression doing something funny to his insides. "I happen to know that you're incredibly capable. Besides, maybe I also want to give you a reason to stay. I'm busy with my company and used to being alone, but I'd regret not seeing what this is between us."

"Me too, which is why I'm here."

"Now that that's understood, have I told you that

I also find you incredibly sexy?"

She giggled as he moved even closer, his erection brushing against her stomach as his lips found hers. Before long, he had her gasping, clutching onto his head as he ate her out in the steamy shower. Anna's cries filled his bathroom, and he knew he couldn't live without this woman in his life.

***

Anna clasped Jett's hand as they walked into the hotel in Seattle, the bellhop handling their luggage. Jett had been trying to stay updated on work issues throughout the morning, but they'd still talked quietly on the flight. Jett's office had booked them seats in first class, and she'd enjoyed the extra space and perks. Somehow, he'd arranged for an early check-in, which was nice. They'd risen early to catch the flight to the West Coast, and combined with the time change, she was already feeling sleepy.

"We'll drop our bags off, freshen up, and then go sight-seeing for a couple of hours before my meeting. Unless I have to get involved in that other issue I mentioned, the rest of my time here is yours."

"Okay. Hopefully our plans this morning involve coffee."

He chuckled, pulling her close. "Seattle's best," he joked.

His phone buzzed, and Jett spoke in a low voice as he answered. "Understood," he said quietly. "We don't want to miss our chance. Keep me apprised of the situation. I'm about to check in to my own hotel. I've got a meeting over drinks at noon."

He murmured something Anna couldn't hear, and

then Jett was pocketing his phone and sliding his credit card to the hotel front desk.

"Thank you, Mr. Miller," the woman said with a smile. Anna raised her eyebrows, but Jett simply smiled, taking his card back. He got the key cards to their room and escorted Anna to the elevator, ducking over to speak into her ear.

"I didn't mention it, but the team often travels under aliases."

"Sounds suspicious," she joked.

"It's for our own safety," he said.

It wasn't the first time Jett had said what they did was dangerous, and Anna wondered again what he wasn't telling her. Providing security detail for officials obviously required certain measures of protection. Jett had explained over the weekend that he kept weapons at his home and office. His team was traveling for something related to Shadow Security as well. She didn't know the first thing about playing bodyguard, but if the men who worked for Jett were as fit as him, she assumed their charges were in capable hands. Jett had said he was here on business, too. "Does the person you're meeting with later know your real name?" she asked quietly.

Jett nodded as the elevator doors closed. "He does. My government contacts are all aware. Doing business with them doesn't require a pseudonym. Sending my men on assignment, however, is a different story. We don't want them tracked by the wrong people. We don't leave paper trails. I get used to checking in under an assumed name and had this hotel room booked as such."

"Did you put my name on our hotel reservation?"

"Yes I did, Mrs. Miller," he said with a wink.

Her lips parted in surprise, and then doors opened. They walked into the hall, Anna feeling more and more bewildered.

"I want to protect you, too, sweetness. I already told you that."

"I know, I just—I didn't think that's what it meant." She shook her head in amazement. Jett really did operate in an entirely different world than her. "You said you've got a meeting today. Are you on some assignment, too?"

"No, sweetness. It is just a meeting. The assumed name is only a precaution."

A small hint of uneasiness washed over her. She trusted Jett. She believed what he'd told her. Aside from her friends' own Internet searches, she'd looked up Shadow Security herself. Jett's name was listed— his real name. She noticed he didn't have a photograph on the website, but aside from that, the services they provided were what he'd explained to her. Then again, he'd also said not everything they did for the government was published online. And why hadn't he mentioned booking the hotel under a different name?

They walked down the hall, the bellhop already waiting at the door. Jett handed him a folded bill and then took their bags in himself. She only had a small carry-on suitcase. Compared to Jett's duffle bag, however, she almost felt like she'd overpacked. Jett walked into their hotel room first, his gaze sweeping the space.

"Are you always so cautious?" she asked.

"Yes. Especially now that I have you traveling with me." She paused in surprise, staring at him. "I don't mean to frighten you," he said. "In my line of work, it pays to be careful. My home is secure, but when we're out in public together, I'm aware of my surroundings."

Anna let out a breath. "Okay."

Jett held out his hand. "Come look at this view," he said. She could tell he was trying to distract her but crossed the room to the balcony doors and then gasped. In the distance was a snow-capped mountain peak, towering over the city. The sky was clear blue, tall buildings surrounded them in the hotel, but the breathtaking portrait of nature in the distance was simply stunning.

"That's Mt. Rainier," Jett said in a low voice. "It's over fourteen thousand feet tall and is the highest volcanic peak in the contiguous United States."

She let out a breath. "It's incredible. You don't get views like that in Manhattan."

Jett's muscular arm snaked around her waist, pulling her close. She could smell the pine scent of him mixed in with a hint of spice—pure male. "No, you don't," he said. "I bought a cabin here in Washington, like I mentioned. We won't have time to get there on this trip, but we'll come back to see it. I'd love to take you there."

"I already told you I can't ski very well," she said, suddenly feeling nervous.

Jett's lips pressed against her temple. "I'll teach you. I think this might be the first time I've seen you nervous, Anna. I'd never make you do something you didn't want."

She leaned against him, letting him take her weight. She knew that even without his saying so. Still, it was sweet of him to reassure her. "You do realize you're more adventurous than me," she said, glancing up at him. "I'm impulsive, as you probably gathered, and sure, I'll jet off to a tropical resort at a moment's notice. But skiing? I'll try, but I probably can't keep up with you."

"If skiing turns out not to be your thing, we can have other adventures together."

"Hopefully you're not interested in mountain climbing," she said dryly.

He burst into laughter. "I did some sky diving, repelling, and other adrenaline-junkie stuff in my Army days. It's not like they roll out the red carpet for the Special Forces. We infiltrated enemy camps by any means necessary. But don't worry, I won't expect you to do any of the thrill-seeking activities I have. If you ever change your mind and want to, however—"

"No way!" she hastily said.

Jett chuckled, his lips pressing against her head once more. "I'm fine with tropical resorts, Anna. Or sightseeing in Paris. Or staying cozy at my cabin."

She looked up at him, still feeling slightly uncertain. "Are you though?"

He turned her to face him, looking deep into her eyes. "I never bring women back to my home. I don't introduce them to my team. I don't fly them across the country days after we've met just to spend time together on a quick getaway. It's you, Anna. I want to be with you. Whether that involves dinners in Manhattan, weekends away, or watching you knit—"

She wrinkled her eyebrows. "Knitting? Really?"

He grinned at her, his eyes twinkling in amusement. "I don't know what all your skills are. Maybe you want to knit me a cock sock or something."

She burst into laughter, playfully swatting at him.

"A cock sock? Is that what I think it is?"

His husky laughter filled their hotel room. "It is. One of the guys gave Ford one as a joke last year. He was on a job outside for hours and kept complaining about his balls freezing off."

Anna wiped tears from her eyes. "My God. Please tell me he doesn't wear it."

"God, I hope not. I never actually asked, to be honest. That's one detail I don't need to know about him."

"Well, I definitely don't knit, and even if I did, I wouldn't be making you some balls warmer."

He chuckled, his hands sliding from her waist down to her ass, where he gently squeezed. "I'll have to rely on you to keep me warm instead." He moved closer and kissed her, their breathing growing heavy. She could feel his erection pressed against her, but he pulled back. "Why don't you get whatever you need, and we'll go do some sightseeing. They'll be plenty of time in bed tonight for us to enjoy one another," he joked, waggling his eyebrows.

"Promise?" She pouted playfully at him.

"I'll give you so many orgasms, we'll have to muffle your cries with a pillow. Don't want to disturb the other guests," he said with a wink.

She smirked and glanced out the window again, finally looking back at him. It was impulsive to rush off to Seattle with Jett. She didn't even remember the last trip she'd taken with a man. It felt right though. Real. "You're awfully cocky," she joked.

"It's served me well so far," he replied. "We'll have our alone time later on, sweetness. But now that we're here in Seattle, I intend to show you the city."

Chapter 16

Snagging Anna's hand as they headed back to their hotel, Jett's lips quirked. They'd talked over a leisurely breakfast and walked around some of this part of Seattle, exploring. He'd had to check his text messages several times but was hoping his men had things under control involving the situation with Amir. Now Anna was making up silly stories about people they passed on the street.

"That one," Anna said, nodding toward a woman in a business suit who stepped out of a cab. "She's late for work this morning because she's having an affair with her secret lover who's also her car mechanic."

He chuckled. "Why's she need a cab then? He must be a damn lousy mechanic."

"A lousy mechanic but an amazing lover," she joked.

Jett burst out laughing. "I had no idea you had such a vivid imagination."

"Oh, I can be quite inventive when I want to be." She looked up at him with a smug smile. "Maybe someday we'll have to play patient and nurse. I have a sexy nurse Halloween costume now that I think of it."

"You as a sexy nurse? I'm intrigued."

"Seriously though, I blame Ashleigh. She's an author. We used to make up stories about people we saw back in college and when we were roommates. Usually, hers were much better than mine. I got her good though once. Taking my story-telling skills to the next level, I made an online dating profile for her. It was amazing. I gave her all kinds of ridiculous hobbies and implied she was looking for a husband. She was furious," Anna admitted.

"Was she looking for a boyfriend?"

"Nope. I decided she needed one though."

"How considerate of you," he said, eyeing her in amusement.

"I know, right?" Anna asked. "She had tons of responses. I probably shouldn't have used her real photo. You couldn't really see her face, but it was a nice bikini shot."

"Jesus," Jett muttered. "You shouldn't post your personal photos online."

"You wouldn't want to see my bikini pictures?" Anna teased.

Jett growled and tugged her closer to him. "I wouldn't want anyone else to see them."

The sweater dress Anna had on today perfectly hugged all her curves. She'd changed into it back at the hotel earlier, and Jett was having a tough time keeping his hands to himself. The tall boots she wore clung to her shapely legs and gave her a few inches of height. When they'd been waiting for a cab earlier, he'd pulled her back against him so she could feel just how much he enjoyed that dress. She'd giggled as she'd felt his erection but pulled away, smirking. He'd been the one to tell her they'd have time later for that, so it served him right. It didn't stop him from wanting her though.

Fifteen minutes later, Jett deposited Anna back in their hotel room and then hailed a cab to meet his government contact at a nearby bar. It wasn't ideal bringing her along with him on this trip. Jett wanted to stay with her, enjoying the city. He'd come here for work though, and it couldn't be put off. Although she hadn't minded, he still didn't like leaving her behind.

Jett gave the driver the address, and then they pulled into traffic. His phone buzzed with a call as Ford's name flashed on the screen.

"Any updates?" he asked in a clipped tone.

"Negative, boss. I went back to his room this morning in hopes he'd come for his suitcase and shit but nothing so far. Sam is planning to wait at the airport in case he shows for his scheduled flight later. I've talked with the IT guys about the traces they're running. Amir must be paying in cash because he hasn't made any credit card transactions."

"What about his phone?" Jeff barked.

"Nothing. He must've turned it off. It hasn't pinged anywhere since yesterday morning."

"When he left the hotel. Damn it," Jett muttered. "I was hoping for better news."

"I searched through some of his things, but they don't give any indication as to where he went. His laptop and phone are gone, presumably still with him from yesterday. I wish I brought more equipment. He either had eyes on his hotel room yesterday or has cameras in here. It's too much of a damn coincidence otherwise."

"Agreed. He knew you were there," Jett ascertained.

"He must have. Why divert from his routine otherwise? I'm going to head back in there and search the place thoroughly for hidden cameras. There's got to be something we're missing here, boss."

Jett clenched his jaw. This was not the news he wanted. The government had provided Jett with Amir's name, schedule, and flight info. All his men had to do was snatch him, and the guy had up and vanished. "I've got a meeting but will touch base with you afterward. Keep me posted."

"Roger that, boss."

Jett handed the cab driver some cash and exited the vehicle, heading toward the bar. Fucking Amir. This should've been an easy snatch, and here they couldn't even get eyes on the target. Jett ordered a whiskey, eyeing his watch. His DOD contact wasn't the same official who'd tasked them with exfiltrating Amir. Jett was anxious to learn about the missing American women. He also needed to finish and shelve this current op. Nothing was ever as simple as planned.

"You're late," he said at five after noon as his government contact showed.

The man chuckled. "Don't worry. I'll be brief. This has all the materials you'll need to look into that sex-trafficking ring in South America. It's tricky, because the cartel has ties to the government, and

State doesn't want to make waves. There are other issues at stake."

"So you need us to get our hands dirty." Jett opened the portfolio, quickly thumbing through the papers. These was a dossier on the cartel leader. Pictures and profiles of the missing American women. Maps. Schematics of the compound. He met his contact's gaze. "Why couldn't you send this through an encrypted file?"

The man leaned closer. "Not everything's on paper. Some US officials are making use of the women there—underage, American women. They're taking advantage of them—using the women caught up in the sex-trafficking ring for their own purposes. Your team will rescue the women, but we need details on how many US government officials are involved in this dirty deal."

"Fuck," Jett muttered. He scrubbed a hand over his jaw, irritation roiling through him. There would always be evil men in this world who took advantage of others, who relied on their money and power. Corruption and evil could rise to the highest offices in the land. It was disgusting enough to know they'd use women held by sex traffickers against their will, but to learn that some were underage? That they had no choice but to service these men? His blood boiled. Jett didn't think fondly of men like that, who intimidated the weak and took advantage of the situation.

"What do you need? A list of the pricks involved?" He finished his whiskey, the smooth liquid burning down his throat.

"Affirmative. We'll handle them. The rescue of the women is the priority, but I want names."

"You got it."

"I'm catching a flight to Asia in a few days. That contains everything you'll need to get started," his contact said, eyeing the folder. "Let me know if anything is unclear."

Jett nodded. "It looks to have all the information I need. We can do further research as well if necessary. I'll handle it."

Jett's contact rose, shaking his hand. He pulled some cash from his wallet, dropping it on the bar to cover Jett's drink. "Hope it wasn't too much trouble coming out to Seattle for such a quick meeting."

Jett shook his head. "No trouble at all for an old friend. I'll be in touch."

Jett watched as the DOD official walked out of the bar. His gaze landed back on the folder. Worming out how many US government officials were involved in this would be tricky. He'd need men on the ground to start surveilling. Records of the comings and goings of the officials. They'd need to determine the condition of the women before a rescue could take place. What a clusterfuck. Certainly, the men using the women in the worst way possible would realize when they simply vanished. He needed to ferret them out before they realized what was going on.

He pulled his phone from his pocket, calling Anna. His mind was already churning with all the complications this next mission would involve. And they still needed fucking Amir.

"Hi there, sweetness," he said as she answered, his mind instantly calming at the sound of her voice.

"Hi baby," she said. "All done with your meeting already?"

"I am. I need to touch base with my team again, but I'll be back soon. I made lunch reservations for us."

"You did?"

He chuckled. "Well, technically, I had Lena make us a reservation while we were in the air this morning. She also arranged some other things for me. After lunch we're going up in the Space Needle."

"Really? All the touristy stuff," Anna joked. "However do you stand me?"

His lips quirked. "It's not a hardship. I'll be back at the hotel in fifteen minutes to pick you up. Sorry that I had to leave for the meeting."

"It's okay," she assured him. "That's why we're here, right? I sort of crashed your business trip."

"That you did, but I'm not complaining." Jett stood up from the barstool, heading out into the sunny day. "The restaurant is supposed to be amazing, so I hope you're hungry. I'll see you soon." He walked down the city block after they said goodbye, scanning the streets out of habit. There was a cab a block away at a red light, but he could walk back. His phone buzzed in his pocket, and he pulled it out to see one of his IT guys calling.

"I think I found something, boss," West Renken said, his gruff voice rumbling over the line.

Jett was instantly alert. "Tell me."

"I hacked into the security cameras at the hotel as you requested. The facial recognition software wasn't picking up Amir, but then I started manually reviewing the footage from the back of the building. There was some unusual activity when the garbage was brought out early yesterday morning."

"Shit," he muttered. "Amir hid with the goddamn trash?"

"Yes," West said. "Or someone resembling him did. When the workers were rolling it out to the dumpster, a man climbed out. It's hard to get a clear image, but the man absolutely resembles Amir."

"What time?" Jett asked urgently.

"Oh-seven-hundred Pacific time."

"God damn it. Ford was in his hotel room then. This isn't a coincidence. Maybe Amir had cameras inside and saw Ford there. Thanks for the update. I need to inform the others." Shaking his head, he quickly called Ford as he hurried down the block. This changed everything. Amir wouldn't return to the hotel at all if he knew they were watching him. He'd probably change his damn flight as well. Jett wanted his team to grab him and deliver him to the Feds wrapped in a fucking bow, and somehow this asshole knew they were watching him.

Jett cursed as he hurried down the street, updating Ford about the surveillance footage when he answered.

"There are cameras in his room," Ford confirmed. "I just started another search. I don't have any equipment for that type of thing with me, so it'll take some time to search everything. He had a camera hidden across from his bed."

"What? You're kidding me."

"Negative. Like I said, it was tricky without our equipment to detect the camera signals, but I found one. I took out the memory card and was able to see the footage on my laptop. The camera wasn't for maintaining security in his room. He was bringing women there for sex and secretly filming them."

"Jesus Christ. The conference was only a few days. How many women could he have been with?"

"A new one each night. He must've brought them back from those nightclubs. The Feds had eyes on him to follow his movements, but maybe he had the women meet him here and they were unaware. This is some raunchy stuff."

Jett blew out a sigh. "So he saw you in his room from the hidden camera he had planted, and he split."

"He's got to leave Seattle at some point. Even if he realizes that he's being watched, he lives in D.C. I doubt he's planning to drive across the country."

"It's a problem that he knew you were there," Jett said. "Damn it. I had plans this afternoon with Anna, but I'm going to need to track Amir instead."

"Wait, you brought a woman with you to Seattle?" Ford asked, confused.

Jett muttered a curse. "I did. It was a coincidence that my DOD contact was here. That meeting was brief. You and Sam should have been long gone had everything happened according to plan."

"Well this throws a wrench in things," Ford said.

"Damn straight. Meet me in my hotel room. I doubt he'll go back to his." Jett rattled off the address and room number. "Unfortunately, Amir knows what you look like. Sam can wait at the airport, but hell. I'm going to step in. Amir will be watching for you. We've wasted time expecting him to show up at his own hotel. He's known he's being watched since yesterday morning."

"Roger that boss. I'll see you in twenty."

Jett slipped his phone back into his pocket and crossed the intersection as the light changed. He was going to have to cancel lunch with Anna—cancel their plans for the day. He scrubbed a hand over his jaw. He needed to find Amir.

Chapter 17

"Good afternoon!" Anna said as Ashleigh answered her cell phone. Although it was noon in Seattle, it was already three back in New York. Anna pictured her best friend at her place in Brooklyn, writing at her laptop, a steaming cup of coffee on her desk. "You'll never guess where I am."

"Jett's house."

Anna smiled, her gaze flicking to the windows and Mount Rainier in the distance. "No, but I'll give you a hint. It involved an airplane."

"What? You did not quit your job and fly off on vacation somewhere. Anna!"

"Well, just a quick trip," Anna admitted. "Jett had some business in Seattle, so I came along. We're doing a little sight-seeing later this afternoon and will stay overnight. But listen—this weekend. I really want you to come meet him."

"In Seattle?" Ashleigh asked, bewildered.

Anna laughed. "No, we're flying home tomorrow. I want you to come up to Jett's house. He'll arrange for a car or have his assistant send one. It's only an hour north of the city. I know you'll like him."

"Oh my gosh," Ashleigh groaned. "I still can't believe you just up and went to his place."

"Well, it's not forever—yet," she quickly amended. Yes, it was a bit crazy to have moved in with him days after first meeting, but that was life. You never knew what would happen.

"Geez. I write romances, but I didn't expect you to fall head first into one of your own. Of course I'll come meet him, I'm just still in a bit of shock over all of this."

"Yeah, me too. I feel like I'm on vacation this week. Everything hasn't really sunk in yet. My boss offered me my old job back for twice the salary."

"Crap," Ashleigh said with a laugh.

"I know, but it's too little too late. I was ready to get out of there. Jett actually offered me a job, but I don't know. Sleeping with the boss isn't a good idea. And Ash—the sex is off-the-charts spectacular."

Ashleigh burst into laughter. "Oh my God. Only you. You're living your own little fairy tale right now. He owns a successful business, jets off at a moment's notice. He's rich, charming, presumably handsome. When can I expect to babysit your little rugrats?"

"Ha ha. I've got no idea if he wants kids. This is all new, but I really like him. He's not like the men we're used to in Manhattan with designer suits and an unhealthy obsession with the stock market. He's real."

"Well, let me know when you get back to New York. I'm sure I can fit meeting Jett into my busy schedule," Ashleigh joked.

"I will. Talk soon, okay?"

Anna ended the call, smiling. It had been a glorious morning to stroll around the city. They'd had an amazing breakfast with plenty of coffee and delicious food. Jett had lunch plans for them. And he'd been sweet to her today, holding hands as they walked around, stealing a kiss every once in a while. For such a gruff man, he was gentle when he wanted to be.

She shivered. He was also commanding and confident in bed. A dangerous combination.

The keycard sliding in the door and tiny beep let her know Jett was back. She was smiling as he came in, and then her face fell as she caught his expression. He was tense, his shoulders stiff and hands fisted. "What's wrong?" she asked.

"One of my men is on his way over," he said grimly. "They were here in Seattle for another matter, but there's been a complication."

"Oh."

He crossed the room toward her, and she could see the concern in his eyes. "We're going to have to skip our lunch reservation. We can order room service while I go over things with Ford. He'll be here in twenty minutes or so."

"Ford?"

"One of my guys. He works at Shadow Security headquarters. He was here for work, but I need to step in."

"What do you mean?"

Jett briefly pulled her into his embrace, looking into her eyes. "He'll stay here with you, sweetness. I need to go out and look for someone. It's complicated."

"So…no sightseeing with you."

"I'm afraid not. It's a coincidence that I was here in Seattle while my men were, but it's an urgent matter that needs to be taken care of. I'll likely be tied up for the rest of today."

"Um, okay. I guess I shouldn't have come along on a work trip after all," she said, pulling back. She'd just been bragging to Ashleigh about how amazing Jett was. She couldn't help but feel slightly hurt.

He was watching her carefully, his gaze softening. "I'll make it up to you," he promised. "I know this wasn't the trip we envisioned, but hopefully by tomorrow we'll have some time to explore."

"So…what? I should just go off on my own today?" She pulled away, beginning to feel a little frustrated. Jett was always having to take calls, conduct business. He'd gone into his office on Sunday for a meeting. He was up in the middle of the night. He'd been working on the plane. She didn't have an issue with him going to his business meeting earlier—after all, that had been the point of this trip. But even when they were together, his mind was on work. He'd switched their plans again at a moment's notice.

"Anna," he said, following her across the room. Tears smarted her eyes. It was silly, really. She'd known he was here on business. She felt sort of like an afterthought though—his shiny new toy to play with, until work came up. No, he didn't answer his phone during sex like her ex had, but still. He kept up and leaving. It was clear what his priority was.

She walked into the bathroom, surprised that he was following her. After spending every moment together for days, she really just wanted some space.

Sniffling, she swiped at her eyes. She wasn't going to cry over this. His work was more important than her. The message was clear. She'd known him for mere days, so what did she expect?

Jett's big hands landed on her hips, and he was pulling her back against him. "Are you crying?" he asked softly.

"I'm fine."

"Sweetness…." He brushed her hair to the side, kissing the back of her neck. Instantly, her nipples pebbled and arousal pooled at her core. Damn her body for betraying her. "I'm sorry to keep getting tied up with work. I want to spend time with you," he said, lightly nipping at her neck. "I want to spend hours exploring the city together. I want to spend days finding out what you like, learning every single thing about you. I want you."

His breath was hot on her skin, his body pressed against hers. Jett was hot and hard behind her, all muscle and male. The heat of his body surrounded her. He kissed her neck again, swiping her skin with his tongue as she gasped. Jett edged her forward, their gazes locking in the bathroom mirror. The air between them was thick and erotically charged. Jett's hands slid to the hem of her fitted sweater dress, his thick fingers trailing up her bare thighs.

He tugged her sweater dress to her waist, revealing her thong. Jett gripped the strap, tugging it up so it pulled against her pussy. "Are you wet for me?" he asked huskily. She whimpered but nodded, and then Jett bent her over the counter. He was unzipping his pants as he leaned over her, kissing her softly and whispering sweet words in her ear. Jett pulled her thong down with one hand, sliding his fingers through her arousal-drenched folds with the other. She gasped as he circled her clit with one finger. He moved closer and then entered her from behind in one smooth movement as she moaned. It was sudden and possessive. A claiming. His body pinned hers down, in complete control. His words were gentle though. Soothing.

"Sweet Anna," he murmured, holding still as she relaxed to accommodate his size. His hands were everywhere—calming, caressing. His lips moved against her hair. "You have no idea what you do to me."

She cried out as his fingers caressed her clit. He was thick and hard, filling her completely. He strummed her swollen nub expertly, like they'd been lovers for years. He was in absolute control, and she was helpless to the way he made her feel. Jett slowly moved in and out of her body, stroking every nerve ending inside her. Warmth flooded through her, her body already coiling tight.

"Say you're mine," he ordered.

Anna gasped as he began moving faster, his fingers teasing her.

"Say you're mine, sweetness," Jett said again. "Only mine."

Her orgasm came out of nowhere. One moment, Jett was urging her on, and the next, she cried out his name, gasping and clutching onto the counter as her inner walls clamped down around him and she exploded.

"Anna," he groaned, thrusting harder. Jett stiffened and then came as well, grabbing some tissues to clean up as he pulled out. She was still panting and met his gaze in alarm as someone knocked loudly on the hotel room door. Jett tugged her dress down, but her thong was still around her ankles. He tucked himself back in, zipping up his pants. His kiss was bruising, pleading for her to understand. "Take whatever time you need," he said. "That's Ford." He pulled the bathroom door shut behind him as he left, giving her privacy to right herself. She heard voices as the hotel door opened, and she stood there staring at herself in the mirror—cheeks flushed, hair a mess, and eyes wide. Despite everything that had happened, she was completely falling for this man.

***

Anna's cheeks heated as she finally came out of the bathroom ten minutes later. She'd cleaned up and righted herself, but Jett's sudden claiming of her and confession was astounding. He'd said Anna didn't know what she did to him, but Jett was wrong. She felt it, too, whatever magnetic force kept pulling them together. Even when she'd been upset, his touch and words had been what she craved, what she needed. It was Jett that held all the control. He could destroy her if he wanted, she was already so wrapped up in him. How could she fall so quickly, so deeply, for a man she'd just met? He made her feel things she never had before and was so attuned to her it was almost frightening.

The men were talking in hushed tones, and she was absolutely positive the guy on Jett's team knew what they'd been doing before he'd arrived. Not that Jett would kiss and tell, but the man had knocked on the door moments after—

She bit her lip. There was nothing to be embarrassed about. She was literally staying at Jett's house. Of course, the men who worked for Shadow Security would assume they were romantically involved. Still, she couldn't help but feel slightly out of sorts. Where did she fit in Jett's strange world?

A large man looked up at her as she walked into the hotel room, his gaze assessing.

"Ah, this is Anna," Jett said, crossing the room toward her. It was oddly sweet. They were busy, but he was coming to make sure she was comfortable. It was a gentlemanly thing to do minutes after he'd pulled her dress up and taken her bent over the bathroom counter. Would it always be this way with him? This irresistible mix of passion and normalcy?

His lips briefly brushed against her temple, and his large hand landed on the small of her back. She'd righted her dress and of course had her thong back on. Anna was certain Jett was also thinking of their heated moment of passion. Secretly, she loved that he couldn't keep his hands off of her. She just hoped she would eventually be a priority to him if they did have an actual relationship. Was it just chemistry between them now? She hated the uncertainty she'd begun feeling. Anna was a confident woman, but she didn't like knowing his work had to always come first. This was hardly the conversation to have at the moment.

"I'm Ford," the large man said as he stood, reaching out a muscled hand. He was bigger than Luke, who she'd met yesterday. Slightly taller than Jett. She shook his hand, wondering if every guy who worked for Jett was this fit.

"Why don't you sit down," Jett said, guiding Anna to a chair. "We're just finishing up." Jett exchanged a glance with his teammate. "You can speak freely in front of her."

Ford nodded. "I got confirmation that he didn't fly out of Seattle. Unless we can locate him, however, we're fucked."

"I'm still hoping he shows up for his scheduled flight. Like I said earlier, he'll recognize you. I'll have to go to the airport with Sam. The guys arranged for another pilot at the military airstrip. You'll stay here with Anna at the hotel."

"Sure thing, boss."

"What?" she asked. "What do you mean?"

Jett clenched his jaw. "I've got to locate someone. Ford will stay here with you today. If all goes well, I'll be back this evening." He shot another look at Ford, and Anna wondered what he wasn't saying. Clearly, they weren't speaking entirely freely in front of her despite his statement moments ago. Anna watched as both men's phones buzzed, and then suddenly Jett was jumping to his feet.

"I've got to go," Jett said urgently. "I can be there in thirty minutes. He's been located."

"But—"

"Ford will stay here with you."

She walked over to Jett, trying to stop him. "What's going on? I don't need some babysitter or bodyguard here with me. If you have to go find someone, I'll be fine. I'll just go sight-seeing myself. I live in Manhattan for God's sake. I can find my way around Seattle."

Jett looked at her, frowning. "No. I want you to be safe, Anna. Just stay here so I don't have to worry about you today. I care about you."

"But you keep up and leaving me," she said,

growing flustered. "I don't even understand what's going on."

"I'll explain later. Promise me you'll stay with Ford."

She blew out an exasperated sigh. "Fine. I'll stay with him. Whatever."

Jett pressed his lips together, eyeing her before he nodded. He turned away to grab some things. Jett spoke in hushed tones to Ford and then was rushing out of the hotel room, his heated gaze landing on her as he glanced back over his shoulder. He didn't stop though. He didn't kiss her goodbye or say anything further.

The hotel door clicked shut behind him.

Chapter 18

Jett cursed under his breath as he hustled out of the hotel and onto the busy Seattle street. Anna had looked almost wounded when he'd abruptly changed their plans for the day. He hated that the operation his Shadow Ops Team was running had crashed into his personal life. What were the chances he'd be here in Seattle with a woman when the shit hit the fan? The meeting earlier about their next mission had gone down as smooth as the whiskey he'd ordered.

But the exfiltration of Amir? Damn it all to hell.

Jett lifted his phone to his ear, calling his IT guy West at Shadow Security. "You're positive his phone pinged off a tower near the airport," Jett said.

"Yes, boss. Less than ten minutes ago. I hacked into the flight databases to search the records and passenger manifests. He hasn't changed his flight that's scheduled at nineteen hundred, but that doesn't mean shit. He could have booked something sooner under an alias."

"I hear you," Jett muttered, hailing a cab.

It fucking killed him to leave Anna in the hotel room with Ford. He trusted his former Army buddy with his life—with Anna's life—but that didn't mean he wanted to leave her alone in a strange city. Yes, she was a grown woman and capable of taking care of herself, but he'd flown her out here. He was responsible for her. The chemistry always simmering between them was palpable. Irresistible. They'd flirted this morning in the hotel room. Over breakfast. Walking back to their hotel. When she'd pulled away from him in tears, it was all he could do to soothe and reassure her. Their bodies connected as one was like a goddamn religious experience. And he wasn't a religious man. It was her. Pure Anna.

Jett wasn't sure he could forget the look in her eyes as he took her in front of the bathroom mirror. For the briefest of moments, it was like he could see right into her soul—pure, vulnerable, beautiful. She'd let him into her body and heart, and he'd taken a meeting with his teammate and rushed away for business—for a job.

He instructed the cabbie to drive him to Seattle-Tacoma International Airport, clenching his fist. If she was still speaking to him after this, he'd have to explain everything—the extent of the missions he ran. Hundreds, if not thousands, of lives were at stake here. Amir's malicious plans for acts of terrorism at U.S. universities could end the lives of so many. They needed to get him out of the country for questioning. If he made it back to his embassy beforehand? It was over. He had the information the government needed to stop these acts of terrorism.

"Sam is already in place, boss," West said. "He

hasn't spotted Amir at the airport yet, but I'm trying to see if I can pinpoint his location. I'm going to hack into the cameras and find him to speed things along."

"Roger that. I'll be there soon. Sam and I will nail this asshole down." Jett's hand absentmindedly slid to his sidearm. Getting through security would be a bitch. It wouldn't be the first time he'd circumvented airport security though. Sam was already on the inside, monitoring various gates that had flights to D.C. today. They needed specifics though—Amir's exact location. They needed to end this.

"I'll call you when I have more information," West said.

"Got it." Jett ended the call without saying goodbye, grabbing his burner phone.

Looks like Christmas is coming.

His team back at headquarters had found another pilot for hire. Thank fuck Luke and Nick knew who to contact and which wheels to grease. The pilot would be on standby for the next eight hours. They just needed to get Amir there and on his way to the Feds at the black site.

His personal phone buzzed, and he frowned at Ford's message.

Ford: *Anna is pissed that you left her with me.*

Jett blew out a sigh. He already knew she was upset. She deserved a man who could give her his complete attention, but he didn't think he could let her go. Whatever was happening between them...it had killed him to see her tears. Anna was quickly becoming the most important thing in his life. Her smiles and laughter, their late-night talks in the dark, their lovemaking. Shit. It was all too soon to be thinking this way. Was he falling in love with her?

He'd known her mere days. That didn't make the feelings coursing through him less real.

He thumbed her a text message.

Jett: *I'm sorry, baby. Stay with Ford. We'll talk tonight when I'm back.*

Jett: *I'll explain everything.*

For the briefest of moments, he began to doubt whether or not he should've headed to the airport. Ford was watching her. She was safe. It was unlike him to ever second-guess himself, but a dark feeling of dread washed over him. She'd be safe with Ford. That was all that mattered at the moment.

***

Anna bristled as Ford tried to make small talk with her. She was stuck in a hotel room on her quick trip to Seattle with a man she didn't even know. "Look Ford," she said, standing up and pacing. "I can't sit here all day. I don't care what Jett said. Seattle is no more dangerous than Manhattan—probably less so. I'm not staying here in this hotel room staring at the walls until he gets back."

The large man scrubbed a hand over his jaw. "I understand why you're upset, but Jett asked me to look after you."

"Well, you know what?" Anna asked, her irritation growing. "He has no right. He's been busy the entire time we've been here. I would've stayed in New York if I knew it would be like this. I specifically asked if his work trip would include time for me."

"He didn't plan—"

"He didn't plan anything," Anna interrupted. "I know. Jett expects everyone to cater to his schedule and adjust their lives accordingly. Well, maybe it doesn't work that way. Maybe this was a mistake," she huffed. Anna turned and grabbed her purse, fuming.

"I won't stop you from leaving, but I'm coming, too," Ford said.

"You're following me."

He lifted a shoulder. "I'll stay out of your way if you want, but I'll be there. I promised him I'd look after you."

"Great. Like my own personal bodyguard. Why can't you just go help Jett with whatever this problem is?"

Ford eyed her carefully, blowing out a sigh. "Some of the work we do is secret. Classified. Jett told you some of that, although I know he didn't share any details. If they've seen my face, there's no point in trying to find our guy. He'll recognize me."

"Jesus. You guys sound like criminals or something."

He stiffened. "Not criminals. We're the ones catching the bad guy."

"That's what Jett is doing now," she said. "He told me he just had a meeting in Seattle, that it was safe for me to come. This is total bullshit."

"He's just trying to protect you," Ford said quietly. "And he did have a meeting. This other stuff didn't go as planned. I was compromised. The target we're after doesn't know what Jett looks like. He was here, so it made sense for him to move in. We can't wait for another guy to fly out."

Anna's face fell, looking at Ford in disbelief. "I can't live like this," she said softly. "I mean, if he's going to rush off all the time and—" She swiped away a stray tear. "Look, I'm going out to lunch. Come with me, don't come, I don't really care. I know he runs a security business, but I don't think he's been totally honest with me about the extent of what he does. I just have to get out of here."

Anna turned, leaving the hotel room. She heard Ford quietly walking behind her toward the elevator, but she didn't care. All of this defied logic. Everything. Jett was out there playing cloak and dagger, just assuming she'd be okay with all of it. What had she gotten herself into in coming to Seattle with this man?

Chapter 19

Jett carefully lifted the HVAC vent in the ceiling of the men's room. He'd crawled through the air ducts, working his way past security and the TSA agents. He needed his weapon to get Amir, and it's not like he could stroll through security without a boarding pass anyway. Sam was inside the terminal and had already secured a rental car using an alias. They'd locate Amir at the gate and escort him quietly off airport property. He didn't like grabbing him here out in the open given the layers of security and cameras everywhere, but it was their last resort. He couldn't fly back to Washington. The Feds had been monitoring him, and it was go time.

He shifted the vent to the side, the metal-on-metal clanging and echoing around the men's room. Testing the strength of the duct opening, Jett grabbed hold and dropped to the ground, landing in front of the urinals. He looked up at the giant hole he'd left in the ceiling. Anyone could access the air ducts now, but he needed to move. Hell. This wasn't where he expected to end up. He'd just flown into the damn airport this morning.

Jett called West, fuming as he strode out of the men's room. "Did you locate which gate Amir's at?"

"Negative. Luke is pulling up Amir's known aliases. I don't see any of those names on the passenger manifests. His phone hasn't pinged again off any cell towers either. He might have turned it off."

"Damn it," Jett muttered. "Get me a list of all flights to D.C."

"Already did. Check your email."

Jett ended the call, swiping the screen on his phone to read his messages. Hell. He and Sam would have to monitor the gates and somehow intercept Amir before he boarded. He just hoped the asshole wouldn't cause a commotion given that his life was at stake. The entire situation was a clusterfuck. Jett strode down the terminal, stopping to grab a coffee and paper. No sense in looking even more suspicious by wandering around the airport with nothing but the clothes on his back.

Unable to stop himself, he texted Ford.

Jett: *How's Anna?*

Ford: *She wouldn't stay in the room. I'm with her.*

"Fuck," he said out loud, causing several people to look over. Jett nodded and moved away, fuming. He'd asked her to do one damn thing for him. She'd be safe with Ford watching her, but he'd felt better knowing she was tucked away safely in their hotel. There were so many things he needed to discuss with her. He'd planned to keep the details of their missions a secret, but in hindsight, he realized that was a mistake. He might not need to tell her everything, but explaining even one of his operations might get her to see the urgency and secrecy they required. He'd fucked up by not revealing everything his team did to her. Shadows and secrets suited a man like him, but if he wanted Anna in his life? He'd have to share some part of himself.

His phone buzzed, and he saw Sam's name on the screen.

"I don't see him, boss. I've searched a couple of gates. We don't even know what flight he's trying to catch."

"I'm on my way to you," Jett said, his gaze sweeping the crowded airport as he ended the call. He hadn't even taken a sip of the coffee he'd purchased. A little girl was jumping and twirling in front of him, and he sidestepped her, hurrying toward Sam. The arrivals and departures board was full. Announcements were coming over the PA system. Two giggling college-aged girls almost bumped into him.

He trashed his coffee, clutching onto the paper instead. He'd be at Sam's side in less than a minute. They'd formulate a plan to monitor multiple gates. They'd get their man. His phone buzzed again, and he realized West had texted all of them.

West: *Amir's phone pinged near the nightclub. He's not at the airport anymore.*

Sam: *Well fuck. Jett and I are thirty minutes away.*

Ford: *I'm ten minutes from there. I'll get him.*

Jett's blood ran cold.

***

Anna paid the waitress, glancing at her barely touched bowl of soup. It was good, but she wasn't in the mood to eat. Hurt and confusion swirled within her. Did Jett really think he could just brush her off every time work issues arose? And why did he expect her to sit around a hotel room waiting for him all day?

Ford was seated across from her, frowning. He hadn't ordered a thing, just kept by her side as she'd sulked. She felt a little bit ridiculous. She didn't need him following her around. She'd snapped at him when he'd tried to pay for her meal. She assumed Jett would be annoyed she'd even left the hotel, but damn it. He had no right to decide how she'd spend her day.

Ford's phone buzzed, and he muttered a curse, thumbing a response back. "I need to drop you back off at the hotel. There's a problem."

"Then go. You don't need to follow me around. I don't care what Jett said about staying with me. It's the middle of the day. I'll be fine."

"Look, he's not going to be happy if I leave you here alone. I've known Jett for years. We served together back in the Army. Have I met any other woman he's been with during the twenty or so years I've known him? That's a negative, because there aren't any."

"Then take me with you," she said impulsively. "Where are we going?"

"No can do," he said, watching her stand up from the table. "Jett would bust my balls if I brought you along."

Suddenly, she burst into laughter. "I thought they already froze off," she joked.

Ford slanted her a look of disbelief.

"It's a long story," she said. "I had to tell him I had absolutely no knitting skills whatsoever. And if Jett insists that we stay together? Then I'm coming with you, Ford."

"Hell no, Anna. This is for your own safety," he argued.

"Maybe you underestimate me. If you leave me here, I'll just follow you. Now I really want to know what's going on. Will Jett be there?"

Ford didn't answer.

"That's what I thought. Let's go."

"Damn it," he muttered as they walked out of the restaurant. "I'm looking for someone but will wait until the others get there to confront him. You have to stay in the cab, Anna. That's nonnegotiable. Jett will already kill me for even bringing you."

"I'll handle Jett. He knows damn well I'd follow you if I wanted. It serves him right for leaving me in the dark. He flew me across the country and didn't even tell me what you guys really do."

Ford hailed a cab, eyeing her. "Look, I don't have time to argue. I agree, you're a grown woman, and he shouldn't be telling you what to do. You can make your own decisions, but I'm warning you, this is dangerous."

"Thank you."

"Did you hear anything I just said?" he asked in disbelief.

"I did, and I agree. I'll make my own choices."

Ford opened the back door to the cab, and Anna slid in, nerves skittering through her. Jett would be pissed as hell that she'd insisted on coming along. What did he expect though? He was the one who told her to stay with Ford, and she was. Problem solved.

He gave the cab driver the address and shot off a quick text. "I'm not telling Jett you're with me yet. We've got other problems to deal with, and that will just distract him."

"Fine. I'll tell him myself when this is over."

"You realize he wanted you safe so he didn't worry about you," Ford said, looking exasperated.

"He has a rather high-handed way of doing things," she muttered.

Ford leaned closer to her, his large frame taking up much of the backseat of the cab. The driver wasn't paying them any attention, talking into his own cell phone as they drove. "I need eyes on the man we've been looking for," Ford said in a low voice. "Jett and Sam are on their way. It's urgent that we stop him before he leaves Seattle."

"Got it," she said, looking out the window as the cab driver took them to a more run-down area of the city. "I won't get in your way." They pulled up to a nightclub that was currently closed—not surprising given it was the middle of the day.

Ford shifted in the backseat, looking around. "Just stay here for a few minutes," he told the driver. "I'm meeting some friends."

"It doesn't open until seven," the driver pointed out.

"I know."

Ford didn't offer an explanation, and the cabbie shrugged. Anna suddenly began to grow nervous. There was no one around on the street, no other cars driving by, and most of the buildings appeared rundown. She'd been so pissed off at Jett's bossiness she hadn't considered it might truly be dangerous to insist she come with Ford.

"Fuck, there he is," Ford muttered as a man appeared near the doorway to the nightclub. "I need to see where he's going. Stay here." He slipped out the back of the cab, leaving Anna there alone.

"The meter's still running," the driver said.

"I know. It's fine."

Ford disappeared around the side of the building as they sat across the street. Was he hoping to go into the back of the nightclub? She jumped as her phone buzzed.

Jett: *Where are you? Please say back at the hotel.*

Anna: *Nope. I'm with Ford.*

Jett: *Damn it. Are you safe?*

Anna:

She screamed as the back door suddenly opened, and a Middle Eastern man pushed his way in. He held a gun to the cab driver's head and yelled at him to drive. Anna lunged for the door handle to let herself out, and the gunman shot at the glass. She screamed again as glass shards fell down around her. The car lurched forward and swerved, nearly crashing into some trash cans, then sped away as the gunman began yelling at both her and the cab driver. Tears filling her eyes, she sent one last text before the gunman took her phone.

Anna: *Help*

Chapter 20

"God damn it!" Jett roared, punching the dashboard. Anger coursed through him as he read Anna's text. She'd gone with Ford to the nightclub? Was she out of her mind? She hadn't even responded yet when he'd asked if she was safe.

Sam glanced over at him before speeding up on the highway. "What is it, boss?"

"Anna went with Ford to the nightclub after Amir. Jesus Christ. I wanted her to stay in the hotel today. I told her we'd talk later on. Now she went with Ford after this asshole? A goddamn terrorist on the government watch list? I'm going to wring Ford's neck for letting her come along."

Sam frowned and glanced over at him. "I don't blame you, but damn. You know Ford can't say no to a woman."

"He damn well better learn how—especially with this woman. Anna can be surprisingly persuasive. I should've just agreed to let her explore Seattle alone. Now instead of visiting a tourist attraction, she's literally walking into a nightmare."

"Not literally. They probably took a cab."

Jett muttered a curse. "I don't know what the hell Ford was thinking. He's already been compromised. If they see him outside the nightclub, it's over. Amir will run."

"ETA is ten minutes," Sam said. "We'll grab Amir, get down to the airfield, and send him on his merry fucking way. Ford and I will escort him straight to the Feds. You'll take care of your woman, kiss and make up or whatever, and we're good."

Jett closed his eyes for a moment, trying to control the anger coursing through him. He wasn't sure if he was angrier at Ford, Anna, or himself. He knew she liked to make her own decisions. Telling her to stay put had no doubt had the exact opposite result. Anna was a firecracker. He loved that about her. And shit. He was falling in love with her no matter how fast it had been. The thought of any harm coming to her was intolerable. He wasn't sure he could bear it if she got hurt. Anna was impulsive, yes, but also innocent and good. He'd seen the worst of the world and couldn't let her encounter that sort of darkness.

If he'd told her the truth about what his Shadow Ops Team did, he had a feeling she'd have listened to him. She'd have stayed where it was safe. This was partly his fault.

His phone buzzed with one last text, and his stomach lurched.

Anna: *Help*

"She's in trouble," Jett said urgently. "Drive faster. She's pissed as hell at me but wouldn't text asking for help if she didn't need it. Something's wrong."

Sam sped up, their exit less than a mile away. He swerved around several cars and ignored their blaring horns, neatly avoiding any collisions. Moments later, he was getting off the highway and taking an exit toward the outskirts of the city.

Jett's phone began ringing, and he saw it was Ford. "What?" he barked.

"I messed up. I went around back to sneak into the nightclub and left Anna alone. She insisted on coming with me, Jett. I couldn't tell her no. Amir must've spotted me. He kidnapped both Anna and the cab driver."

Jett huffed out a breath, anguish and white-hot anger roiling through him. She'd trusted him to keep her safe here in Seattle, and he'd fucked up. He should've stayed with her himself, screw the mission. Jett knew she did things spontaneously. She was also short-tempered when it came to matters she was passionate about. When she'd had enough of her job and boss's demands, she'd quit. Immediately. When she'd been fed up with him, she'd ignored what he told her and left the hotel.

He'd screwed up, too, he realized. Maybe he hadn't physically harmed her, but he might as well have. He'd failed to protect her. He hadn't told her the truth. He hadn't stayed with her today when she was upset. The thought of any harm coming to her was appalling.

"Which way were they headed?" he asked.

"I don't know. I was inside the damn nightclub. I talked to the guy working there, and apparently Amir was looking for a woman. No doubt he was trying to lose us as well by leaving the airport, but he's got some kind of addiction to porn. He's been bringing women back to his hotel all week. Guess he went back for one of them."

"And Anna is with that monster," Jett seethed.

"We'll get her," Ford said. "I borrowed a car from the guy at the nightclub—using the term 'borrowed' loosely. I'm circling around the area, seeing if I can spot them. I already told West to track their phones. If Amir's phone pinged by the nightclub earlier, he might still have it on."

"Shit, shit, shit," Jett muttered, nearly beside himself with worry. "Have him run Anna's phone, too. She texted me that she needed help."

"I'm sorry," Ford said. "I fucked up."

"We'll talk about it later. Our only priority now is her."

He ran his hands through his short-cropped hair, feeling himself spiraling. For a man who always prided himself on remaining in control, he found himself in uncharted territory. He had to tamp down his anger and emotions and focus on the job. Find Amir, and he'd find Anna. When he did, he'd make sure she absolutely knew she was the priority in his life. Losing her was something he couldn't tolerate. He'd stared evil in the face before, but nothing was as terrifying as knowing that same evil had the woman he loved.

With luck finally on his side for the first time during this damn op, a cab came speeding toward them. One window was shot out, and Sam fishtailed as he tried to cut them off. The cab driver slammed on the brakes to avoid hitting them, and then Amir was jumping out of the cab, Anna in his clutches. He shot the cab driver point blank, pulling Anna into the street with him.

Jett roared in anger and jumped out of their rental car. He and Sam both had their guns drawn and aimed at Amir in an instant. Jett's gaze flicked to Anna for the briefest of seconds to ensure she was unharmed. She was terrified, her face white, tears streaming down her cheeks. His gut roiled at Amir's arm wrapped around her, a gun to her head. His vision tunneled as he focused on Amir's face. The man was sweating, stressed out. Fidgety. He was getting nervous and might accidentally shoot Anna in the chaos. Jett had to stop this right now.

"It's over!" Sam shouted. "Let the woman go. If you cooperate fully, maybe we won't put a bullet in your brain."

Amir began yelling in Farsi, Jett catching only a few words. Jett stepped to the right, he and Sam easing forward. The cab driver was slumped over in his seat, dead. But that bastard Amir had his hands on Jett's woman. His beady eyes shifted, and Jett saw the moment he began to panic.

Amir yanked Anna's hair as she cried out, forcing her to the ground. "Stay back or I shoot her! I have diplomatic immunity in this country. I demand to speak with the embassy.

"You're on the goddamn terrorist watchlist, Amir. There's no embassy trip for you today. We're taking you with us," Jett said calmly. He took a step forward, aiming his gun at Amir's chest. Anna was too damn close for his liking. One movement, and she'd be shot instead of the asshole holding her hostage.

"Stop!" Amir yelled. "Maybe we can negotiate. The woman for my freedom."

"The U.S. government doesn't negotiate with terrorists, asshole. Unfortunately for you, we're not U.S. government." He took one more step, Sam easing closer as Amir's eyes were fixed on Jett. "We run things our way. Get your fucking hands off her." Jett signaled Sam, and as Amir's head turned, Jett shot Amir's kneecap. Anna screamed as Amir fell to the ground, and Sam was on her in an instant, pulling her away from harm. Jett tackled Amir, zip-tying his hands together after he'd gagged and subdued him.

"We need the damn first aid kit," Jett said. He'd tied a tourniquet to Amir's leg so he didn't bleed out, but now this was one more damn complication.

"Ford's on his way," Sam said, holding a crying Anna. "You take your girl. I'll get the kit. We can't have him bleeding out before he's delivered to the Feds."

A moment later, Jett was pulling Anna into his arms. She cried and clung to him, burying her head against his chest. She was trembling against him, and it took everything in him to hold it together. He pulled her even closer, his own body shaking with both adrenaline and relief.

A car door slammed shut, and then Ford was hustling toward them. Jett's men were talking about the remaining logistics after they'd tended to Amir. They'd leave Amir's gun at the scene, incriminating him in the death of the cab driver. If any surveillance footage near the nightclub showed Anna in the cab, Jett would have West wipe it. Ford was a different story, since he'd been seen inside the nightclub.

They'd need a cover story for him if the police came knocking. He'd have his team get on it pronto.

Amir would be long gone when the police arrived, on a plane headed to a black site. With his background, it wouldn't be a stretch to pin the entire carjacking incident on him. Since his prints were all over the gun, there was nothing his men needed to do.

"Leave his wallet," Sam said. "It'll look like Amir ran after he shot the cab driver."

"Put him in the rental," Ford said. "I've got to drop this car back at the nightclub before I get charged with grand theft auto."

Jett turned Anna away from his men, running his hands over her back as she cried. "It's all right. You're safe now," he soothed. "I shouldn't have rushed off earlier."

She looked up at him with tear-filled eyes. "That guy tried to kill me. I thought I was—I just—" She burst into tears again, Jett holding her close.

"It's okay. I'll explain everything later on, sweetness. I'll always protect you, no matter what. Ford will drop us back at the hotel, and then the team will make haste and get this asshole out of here. They can deal with wrapping things up. My only priority is you."

"Jett," she cried softly, clinging to him. It nearly broke his heart. "I was so scared."

"You did so good. You texted me, and I found you. I love you, Anna," he murmured softly. "It's fast and unexpected, but I love you so much. I'll tell you about my job, everything. I want you to be the priority in my life, and I'll do whatever it takes to make that happen."

***

Hours later, Anna emerged from the bathroom at their hotel. She'd taken a long, hot bath alone, telling Jett she needed time to think. They'd talked all evening about Jett's company and the secret missions he ran. She still didn't know the specifics, but she understood enough. Shadow Security fronted his Shadow Ops Team. He really was like some super spy, tasked by the government with secret missions. That description simplified things; she knew. She also knew she'd never have rushed off with Ford if she realized how truly dangerous it was.

Jett's eyes were on her as she emerged from the bathroom wrapped only in her silky robe. "I shouldn't have gone off with Ford today," she admitted.

"I should have told you the truth. I'm still going to hurt him for letting you come along."

She shrugged. "I sort of made him."

Jett stood from the bed, crossing the room toward her. "Does this mean you forgive me?" She searched his face, seeing nothing but love and sincerity there. He looked worried she'd yell at him again, but the reality was, they both needed to trust one another.

"Yes."

He moved toward her quickly, taking her into his arms and kissing her until she was gasping. Jett laid her down on the king-sized bed, untying her silk robe and baring her to his gaze. He kissed her everywhere, his lips and mouth tasting every inch of her body. Anna whimpered and gasped until he finally entered her, making her his once more.

Jett clutched both her hands in one of his, his other hand gripping her leg, further opening her to him. He thrust into her completely, and she cried out at his thickness, at how completely full she was. Jett was watching her expression, waiting for her body to relax. He kissed her face softly as she gave herself to him, the tenderness in his eyes astounding. Jett moved inside her slowly—not chasing down a release, not rushing this. He was making love to her. Making her his in every way imaginable. When his lips met hers, she felt like she might shatter. Emotions were welling up inside of her, ready to spill over. Every inch of their bodies were pressed together, Jett inside her so deeply, it was like they were one.

His fullness stretched her, demanding she yield to him. She was powerless to the intense waves of pleasure washing over her, pulling her under. His tongue traced her lips, seeking entry, and then was pushing inside her mouth, mimicking the movements below.

No part of her was untouched by him. She gasped as he hit some deep, secret spot inside. Anna whimpered and arched beneath him, Jett's body holding her in place. To her shock, he pulled out, flipping her over. Her breasts pressed against the soft sheets, her cheek against the bedding. Jett adjusted her hips and then took her from behind, his thick cock filling her as she clutched the fabric. She couldn't move, couldn't stop the onslaught of pleasure. One hand slid beneath her, strumming her clit. He thrust into her again, faster, and as Jett commanded her body, she cried out her release, her inner walls squeezing around him over and over again.

Anna gasped, completely spent, still clutching onto the sheets. Jett thrust into her once more and stilled, his body stiff as he came. When he rolled her back over, tears filled her eyes. Jett looked alarmed, instantly running his hands over her. "Did I hurt you?"

"No," she said, swiping at the wetness on her face. "I'm fine. Just overwhelmed and—" She squeezed her eyes shut, covering them with her hands.

"Shhh," he murmured, pulling her hands away and collecting her against him. "Sweet Anna, I hate to see you crying."

Tears began to trickle down her cheeks. "It's like I feel too much when I'm with you, helpless and overcome and—" she shook her head, unable to finish.

Jett kissed her tears away, murmuring soothing words. "I feel it too, sweetness. When I'm with you, I feel weak. You carry my heart in your hands and don't even know it."

Anna blinked, looking up at him. His hands moved over her once more, soothing her. He cupped her breast as he kissed her again. "I love you, Anna Dubois. You've been mine since the moment I saw you. It scares me more than anything to be together, more than any dangerous mission I've been on, because you've stolen my heart. I've never given it away before, but it's yours. I'm yours, Anna."

"Jett," she breathed.

Tears smarted her eyes, and he gently kissed them away. "I love you, too," she said. "So much that it scares me and—"

"Marry me," he interrupted, a smile playing about his lips.

"I can't marry someone I've known barely over a week. That's impulsive and crazy even for me," she said, laughing through her tears.

"Maybe I like impulsive and crazy."

She met his gaze, her breath catching.

"Maybe I knew the moment I saw you that my life would never be the same. I knew right then that you were mine. Marry me, Anna Dubois. Let me take you to Paris and give you babies and spoil you forever."

"And what do you get out of it?" she teased.

"You, my sweet Anna. All that I want is you."

Epilogue

"You're kidding me," the deep voice on the other end of the phone growled as Anna and Jett relaxed in his hot tub. "You're getting married? How long have you known this woman?"

"A week," Anna interjected, smiling at Jett. "It's fine. I had my friends thoroughly research your brother. They gave him their seal of approval."

Slate muttered a curse. "You've got to be kidding me."

"Nope, not at all. Jett asked me to marry him, and I said yes. He can be very persuasive."

"Don't I know it," Slate griped.

"She's good for me, brother," Jett said with a smile. "Smart and funny and sexy as hell. Ow," he said as Anna swatted at him.

"You can't say that in front of your brother," she chastised.

Jett's lips quirked, and she giggled, snuggling even

closer to him.

"So where did you two meet?" Slate asked, sounding exasperated.

"In Manhattan. I quit my job and moved in with him," Anna explained. "It's a long story. I also work for him now, too. Can't wait to meet you!" she added with a laugh.

"I'll talk to you soon, Slate," Jett said with a chuckle. "We've got some catching up to do."

"Yes. I can't wait to hear this one."

Jett ended the call and grinned at Anna. "That went well," she said. "Then tomorrow, Ashleigh and Jen are coming over. They'll be mad that we got engaged before you ever met them, but…." She shrugged. "Oh well."

"We're going to pick out an engagement ring tomorrow, too. I never thought I'd propose without a ring, but there you go. Everything about you has surprised me, Anna Dubois." She scooted onto his lap, wrapping her arms around his neck as she faced him. Anna felt Jett's erection rubbing against her core, but it was the loving look in his eyes that completely slayed her.

"And how do I let everyone know you're mine?" she mock complained.

"You'll just have to wait for the wedding. If I have my way, it will be sooner rather than later."

"Mmmm. That could work." She smiled up at him, looking into his dark brown eyes. They still smoldered with possession, but there was another dimension now as well. Love. His hands squeezed her waist as he ducked down to kiss her.

"Have I told you how much I love this bikini on you?" he asked, a gleam in his eye.

"No."

Jett reached up and tugged at the strings behind her neck, letting the top fall and bare her to his gaze. "I do. But I love you in nothing even more." She giggled as he playfully began nipping at her, and then gasped as he sucked one nipple into his mouth.

"Jett," she pleaded.

"I want you once here in the hot tub before I take you to bed," he said roughly, pausing to rest his forehead against her own.

"Yes," she breathed.

"You mean everything to me," he said huskily. He kissed her deeply then, holding her there to him in the swirling water. "I love you, sweet Anna," he murmured.

"I love you, too," she whispered.

The night air chilled the patio around them, the stars twinkled in the dark sky, and she was in her own little version of heaven, right here with the man she loved.

About the Author

USA Today Bestselling Author Makenna Jameison writes sizzling romantic suspense, including the addictive Alpha SEALs series.

Makenna loves the beach, strong coffee, red wine, and traveling. She lives in Washington DC with her husband and two daughters.

Visit www.makennajameison.com to discover your next great read.

Printed in Great Britain
by Amazon

23754750R00108